RESCUE
MISSION

RESCUE MISSION

by JOHN BALL

with the technical
assistance of
Lt. James C. Riley, USN

Harper & Row,
Publishers
New York

LIBRARY OF CONGRESS CATALOG CARD NUMBER: 66–13854

For
Albert J. Franck
who, too, loves airplanes

A glossary of aviation technical terms will be found on page 207.

RESCUE
MISSION

Chapter One /

IN THE VAST SWEEP OF SUN-SOAKED SKY which reached from one sea horizon to the other, the only clouds visible were drifting cumulous masses, which under normal circumstances meant good weather. The breeze was fresh and welcome; it was the kind which can billow inside a man's shirt and suck out some of the accumulated perspiration which makes even light cloth stick to his back when the humidity is high. The few thin palm trees which had been planted around the modest terminal building leaned slightly further than normal away from the wind, but that was all.

Robert Galloway stood well out in the open on the loading ramp with his back to the single maintenance hangar, which was little more than a fair-sized steel shell, and from the force of long habit lifted his face toward the sky. His feet were planted firmly in the crumbling blacktop and his thumbs were thrust under the top of his trousers at his sides while he listened intently to the sounds of the early afternoon.

He heard the familiar pounding of the surf against the heavy rocks which formed the artificial shoreline behind the parking area; he listened to its long-drawn-out rhythm and detected the slight change which had taken place since early morning. He heard the cries of the circling sea birds and watched the way in which they banked against the breeze as they swung out over the water. He heard the occasional rattle of one of the panels which made up the hangar walls and the sound of the wind as it gathered into occasional gusts and swept up tiny dust eddies along the taxiway which led to the single five-thousand-foot runway.

He ignored the sun, which had already burned his face into a parchment brownness and had caused his eyes to wrinkle into a perpetual squint. He ignored the heat to which long years in the Caribbean had accustomed him. He excluded from his consciousness everything but his sense of hearing and concentrated almost fiercely on interpreting the sounds around him. Everything he had worked for for almost thirty years hung on those sounds, and the way he read them would dictate the decisions which he would have to make.

When he had stood for almost ten minutes bareheaded in the burning sun, he turned and began to walk slowly back toward the terminal. In a sense it was his terminal since it was through his almost single-handed efforts that it had been built. He had sketched the original plans, with the compact passenger facility on one side and the small freight depot on the other. He had even included the palm trees, which added the only note of glamour to the otherwise severely practical building. There had been little enough money as it was and he had channeled practically all of it into strictly functional purposes. This was the way he characteristically did things and it helped to account for the fact that he had managed to keep going, one way or another, in the difficult business of operating a shoestring airline.

He was about to walk into his small corner office and check with the command communications set he had there when he heard the familiar drone of twin P. and W. piston engines faintly over the sound of the wind and the distant pounding surf. He turned and waited for the appearance of the DC-3. Presently it came into view, flying with a steady dignity though it was twenty years old and supposedly obsolete by all modern standards. The Air Force still had them in the inventory and there were plenty of pilots to swear that the old Goonie was the greatest bird ever hatched. As it had a hundred times before, the aircraft lowered its wheels, lined up the runway, and began the south-to-north approach. Presently it flared, planted its two fore wheels onto the ground and then eased the tail down as the speed dropped off.

Satisfied with the landing, Galloway went into the office and listened to the latest weather report. Based on what he heard he estimated that he had thirty-six hours in which to get out before the hurricane hit. Her name was Hazel and from all indications she was a big one. Hurricane forecasting had been raised to something approaching an exact science. The Tyros satellites usually spotted them first; after that the high-altitude U-2's came into the picture and got the exact specifications. The guesswork was gone, which was a good thing—now it was simply a case of getting the word in time and moving out before the storm hit. After it had gone you could return and see what was left that could be put back into commission.

There were no passengers on the DC-3 and almost no cargo. That was to be expected since the revenue flight was in the other direction. There was precious little on this small island to attract the visitor despite an optimistic brochure which had been published at the time that the airport had been put into commission. It had some authentic beach and sea views and some copy which promised several impossibilities, such as "faultless cuisine." In the last ten years Galloway had not had a really decent meal on the island; not that he especially cared. His business was keeping the airline going and its four planes in the air; the rest didn't much matter. But someday when he had it made he would sell out, move to California, and eat prime ribs every day for the rest of his life.

Presently the DC-3 pilots came in, short, ageless Scotty Zimmerman, who had no Scottish heritage whatever, and young Wilson, who had dreamed of seeing the far places of the world and was making his start this way.

"We're going to have to get out," Zimmerman began abruptly. "I've been following the reports; the blow is headed right toward us. I think we're going to lose the hangar, but this building ought to be all right."

Wilson nodded his agreement.

"Then we've got some work to do," Galloway declared. "The high-cost spares we'll take with us; the rest, as far as we can, we'll put in here in the freight area and wherever else there's room. As soon as the Connie comes in we can load her up with the extra engines and whatever else looks best."

"Can we do anything about the hangar?" Wilson asked.

"No, I'm afraid not. There isn't time or the manpower to take it down and that would be no guarantee we could secure it well enough to withstand the blow."

Wilson took Galloway's statement as a rebuke although it wasn't meant that way. He closed his mouth firmly and resolved not to speak again until he was spoken to.

"I'll go in town and get some help," Zimmerman suggested. "We'll need manpower to get all the smaller pieces aboard, stuff that we can't handle with the fork lift without pallets."

"I'd rather you stuck around for a little while, Scotty." Galloway looked out the window and drummed his work-hardened fingers on the top of his desk. "Usually labor turns up when we need it and things could get worse a little faster than we expect. Go listen to the surf and you'll know what I mean."

"I heard it," Scotty answered tersely. "Then let's get started with my bird. We'll top her off and move her into the hangar for loading."

As they walked out of the office Galloway sensed the stiffness in his newest co-pilot and casually fell into step beside him. "Is this your first hurricane alert?" he asked in a matter-of-fact voice.

"Yes, it is," Wilson responded quickly. "What can I do to help?"

"First, top off the bird. Take on all she'll hold; the gas will be no good when we come back if the blow really hits. Then help Scotty load up the spares stock. Never mind trying to keep a weight-and-balance sheet, he'll know how much she can carry and when to stop."

"Yes, sir." At once he was eager to begin work, to meet the challenge of the oncoming storm. He thrust out his jaw a little and savored the thought that the first real adventure of his life was about to begin.

The loud phone bell rang and Galloway returned to answer it. The connection was poor as it almost always was, but the welcome words came through in understandable form and he hung up with a sense of relief. He pulled a pair of worn work gloves out of the bottom drawer of his desk before he went out to join the others.

"The birds are O.K.," he reported. "Ned is down for maintenance in Miami. Charlie just called to say that he had the word and would hole in where he is."

Scotty fed the hose up to young Wilson, who stood waiting on the wing. "I wasn't worried; they both know the score. Charlie may catch a trip hauling relief supplies; that usually happens after a good one hits."

"Where's Armando?" Wilson called from up on the wing.

"Saturday afternoon," Galloway answered, "everybody's off. They may come back if they think we need them."

The three men settled down to work. They completed the gassing of the DC-3 and towed it into the hangar, where it sat, nose proudly high in the air, awaiting its next command to duty. Galloway took out a substantial key ring and unlocked the wire door to the spares cage and the tool bin. Then he put on his gloves, picked up a case containing a spare VHF receiver, and carried it himself out to the plane.

In two hours most of the job had been done. The heavier items had been lined up with the fork lift, awaiting the arrival of the four-engined Constellation which was the flagship of the modest fleet. Under Scotty's direction the DC-3 had been loaded with communications gear, instrument cases, and much additional equipment which represented a good share of the dollar inventory of the whole operation. Scotty was engaged in rigging a cargo net over the forepart of the load when the steady controlled thunder of the Constellation could be heard above the rattle of the wind shaking the side panels of the old metal hangar.

Galloway walked out to watch it come in. He always did that; it was his airplane and, while he trusted the crew completely, he loved to watch the big three-tailed bird slide down the glide path and lift her nose high as she flared for her landing. It was his love for flying which had gotten him into this business, and in twenty-eight years he had never lost his ingrained feeling for machines which could take to the air. It was, he thought, his personal secret, but it was well known to everyone who knew him, even very casually.

This time the big graceful bird appeared to be coming in particularly low. As he watched he confirmed the fact that she was well below the glide path, her engines delivering more power than they should in a normal approach. If she was in that position, then there was a reason for it; Herb Stallings, who was flying her, was a complete professional and didn't make careless mistakes. What the reason might be worried Galloway; it could be any one of a number of things or, worse, it might be a combination of two or three of them.

He checked that the gear was down. When he saw that it was he was reassured that at least a pancake landing wasn't in the cards.

The huge plane, which had once been proudly flown by TWA, sank even lower below the normal glide path, and at the same time the engines raised their voices slightly, indicating that more power had been added. Clearly Herb was dragging her in somewhere close to the power curve, keeping her angle as flat as possible. Possibilities flashed through Galloway's mind as he kept up a running calculation between the plane's position and the end of the fairly short runway. Five thousand feet was enough for a Connie, but it did not allow much margin for error. If the brakes were out Herb might have to ground-loop her to keep her from running over into the water, and that could mean trouble in a dozen different ways.

Cautiously the nose of the incoming plane began to rise, much too slowly for a normal landing and too far out to fit standard procedures. But Herb was good and he would know what he was doing. Galloway accepted the fact now that something fairly serious was wrong with his bird. All that he asked was that it be allowed to land safely without serious damage to the airframe or the engines.

Now dangerously low, the Connie lifted her nose a few more degrees and reached for the end of the runway. She came in over the scrub, actually brushing a few of the taller weeds with her landing gear. Then, at precisely the right moment, her engines slacked off and she sank almost imperceptibly onto the concrete, still in front of the numbers and with practically the entire length of the runway before her.

To Bob Galloway's intense relief she began to lose speed as the propellers were reversed and brakes were applied; then she turned with massive shapely dignity onto the short taxiway which led to the ramp. Her port engines burst into a roar and turned her with careful precision onto her assigned parking spot.

Galloway felt a stabbing pain in his chest and realized he had been holding his breath.

He roused himself to action and pushed the boarding stairs unit over to the rear door of the Connie. He usually did that since it saved keeping a ramp attendant on the payroll on Saturday night for that single task. As soon as he had positioned the steps and pushed the lock which held them in place, the door opened from the inside and the huge head and shoulders of Herb Stallings appeared. He was a massive St. Bernard of a man with the calm disposition which sometimes goes with an oversize frame.

"You all right?" Galloway called up.

Stallings emerged from the doorway and came down the steps like a man half his age and weight.

"I'm all right, but the bird isn't. You saw the approach I had to use."

"How bad is it?" There was an edge to Galloway's voice although he tried to keep it casual.

"Stabilizer control boost. It's out. Probably a hydraulic leak. But it will take time to fix. I landed her largely on power and the trim tab."

Galloway gripped the stair railing despite himself. He knew without checking that they had no parts in stock for that kind of a repair; they would have to be flown in. Stallings read his mind and clapped a huge comforting hand on his shoulder.

"I know, Bob, it's rough. The blow is coming on fairly fast and right now, in the shape she's in, I don't know whether we're going to get Connie out of here or not."

Chapter Two /

THE REST OF THE CONNIE'S CREW CAME down the steps, co-pilot Sam Eastman, who was thirty-five and experienced, and flight engineer Toolie Sims, whose mixed parentage showed in his features. Toolie was as good as they came at his trade. Galloway believed that he could take the entire aircraft apart, lay out every one of its tens of thousands of pieces, and then put it all back together again without making a single mistake. Because his mother had been, and was, a Negro he had had trouble finding a berth which measured up to his talents. Galloway had hired him because he knew he was good. He had also sensed that throughout the islands where he was doing business the presence of an important flight crew member such as Toolie would improve the image of his airline. Many of the people whose business he needed to survive had negroid strains and approved of his openmindedness. It was Galloway's good luck that circumstances had made Toolie available to him at a price he could afford to pay; there wasn't a better Connie man around.

With his powerful hand Herb Stallings turned Galloway by the shoulder toward the terminal and the office. "Let's go inside," he proposed. "I want to talk to you a bit."

"I haven't much time for talk," Bob protested.

Herb increased the pressure, indicating that he meant business.

"All right, then," Galloway said. "I can use a break."

As they walked across the blacktop Stallings called, "Hey, Scotty."

Zimmerman looked up, understood, and came to join the party.

Galloway led the way inside the plain concrete building and turned into the stark cubicle that was his office. A single small window looked out toward the water. The walls were bare except for four photographs, a Constellation and three DC-3's each sitting for its portrait as though conscious of the lens and camera. There was a well-worn mahogany-veneer desk, a scarred chair behind it, and a tubing and plastic settee which would hold two.

Just before closing the door Stallings turned his leonine head and with a quick motion indicated that Toolie was to sit in. The flight engineer pulled the door shut behind him and, since the three available seats were already full, turned and leaned easily against the wall.

Although it was Galloway's office and he was the boss of the airline, it was Stallings who took the floor. "Bob, you're going to have to do some hard thinking for a minute."

"Shoot." Galloway leaned back and hooked his legs around the chair.

The big pilot produced a pipe which matched himself in size and took his time packing it with tobacco. "Do you remember just what happened when we bought Connie?" he began.

"Sure. She was available, we needed her, we had the price."

Stallings nodded and struck a match. "Exactly." He spent several seconds getting the pipe going to his satisfaction. "And why did we pick this particular bird?"

"You know damn well; she was the only one we could afford at the time."

A cloud of smoke escaped from between Stallings' lips and drifted slowly toward the ceiling. "And you know why the price was down. She'd been belly-landed once after TWA got through with her and she'd had a maintenance history."

Galloway half rose out of his chair. "I knew that when I signed the contract. Don't try to blame what's happened tonight on me now!"

Stallings ignored it. "Right now she's a damn sick bird. Ask Toolie."

"I don't have to."

"All right, then listen. As she sits she's unsafe to fly. Without a stabilizer boost she can't be handled normally."

"You got her in."

"On the trim tab, yes, but that's strictly emergency procedure." He swung around. "Toolie, what are the chances of getting her fixed in the next twelve hours?"

"None," the flight engineer answered. "It'll take parts we haven't got; the closest are in Miami."

Galloway slapped the top of his desk with the palm of his outstretched hand. "I'm way ahead of you," he retorted angrily. "I'm not going to ask you or anyone else to fly Connie the way she is. I'll do it myself. I'll need Toolie or some-body—I can't do it alone—but I can nurse her up the line and get her into Miami just the way you came in here tonight."

"You're on the wrong heading." Stallings let another thin stream of smoke escape his lips. "If anyone flies her up to Miami I will, but that's not the point. What I'm trying to say to you is that as her captain I'm officially declaring the air-craft unsafe to fly. Every manual there is says so and I've got my flight engineer, and co-pilot, to back me up." He looked toward Toolie, who nodded.

Galloway took a long moment. "What do you expect me to do, leave her here?"

Stallings leaned forward to give added emphasis to his words. "Let me ask you first: would you ever let her go out of here in the condition she's in if the hurricane weren't coming?"

"Of course not!"

"Right. Now, hurricane or no hurricane, Connie isn't fit to fly and you know it. So here's what we do. We secure her to the best of our ability and leave her here."

"No," Galloway said.

"Shut up and let me finish. With this blow coming on everything with wings in this whole area will be headed up toward Miami. The traffic will be saturated. You can't go charging through up there with a bird you can't control properly; it's a violation. They'll have your ticket and every-body's on board. Mine if I fly it."

"That's no problem; if any row is raised the trouble ap-peared on the way up."

"It won't work. Coming in here tonight I talked to airways control and told them I had an emergency situation. So it's already on the record. If they watched my descent on radar, and I'm sure they did, they have a good idea now what it was."

Galloway covered his face with his hands before he looked up. "What the hell am I supposed to do?" he asked.

"Just what the book says," Stallings answered. "Take every precaution you can and leave her here. You've got to. If she comes through, fine; if not, she's insured."

Galloway gripped his hands into fists. "Are you suggesting we try to suck the insurance company into buying us a new bird?"

"Of course not," Scotty Zimmerman cut in suddenly. "Don't you see that if you do try to fly her in her present condition, the insurance company will blame you? No court would hold them responsible if you or anybody else tried to fly Connie with a major power-boost system inoperative."

"If the insurance representative were here right now," Stallings added, "he'd tell you to leave her here. Load up her tanks for ballast, tie her down, and pray for her soul."

"What about the spare engines? She was supposed to haul them out," Galloway said.

"No problem. I'll bring them in here and cover them securely," Toolie answered. "They'll be all right."

"Then all six of us would go out in the three?" It was a childish question, a mental relief valve which eased the pressure.

"Of course," Scotty replied. "No sweat, even with the load we have on board. Two crew, four deadhead."

Toolie, who had had to face some human emotional problems in his lifetime, picked up the threads.

"I have it planned out. I'll tie her down, with the maximum protection possible, well away from the hangar. We've always considered it temporary and it doesn't owe us a dime. With the control locks on, well blocked, and all the tanks full she has a good chance to ride it out."

It was a lie and every man in the room knew it. It was like the ceremony where a dead pope is asked in his own name if he is still alive. No answer is expected, but the question is always put.

"Suppose," Galloway said carefully, "that Connie doesn't make it and the insurance company takes the attitude we had no right to leave her. It would break us."

Stallings shook his massive head from side to side. "I'm the aircraft commander, and unless fraud is suspected my word on the subject is final. There's no fraud and you know it. She has a good chance. If she doesn't make it, then the settlement will get us a much better, lower-time bird on today's market. That's what we buy insurance for, to protect us when we get into a bind like this."

Galloway got up. "I've got to think about it. Meanwhile we've got a lot of work to do. Toolie will need help if he's going to put those engines in here. The way things are, I think we should get out by early morning. I want to take a look at Connie myself."

"By all means," Stallings advised. "I think Toolie should take out the bulkhead door and verify the hydraulic leak, just to be absolutely sure."

"I could take off the cylinder and bring it with us," Toolie suggested.

"No, leave it the way it is unless you can fix it," Galloway instructed. "I might change my mind."

During the night, while they worked, the wind held. The

breakers crashed against the artificial shoreline at the end of the runway with a steady interval; when the moon came center-stage in the night sky its pale light showed occasional flashes of white spray in brief moments of flight before dropping back into the vast anonymity of the sea.

Toolie removed the bulkhead door which concealed the hydraulic power boost for the stabilizer and found the leak even worse than he had expected. He reported that it could not be fixed without the proper parts; both Herb Stallings and Scotty, who also flew the Connie on occasion, verified his findings. Sam Eastman, who wanted to ask questions but had sense enough not to, carefully looked over the system failure in case someone should ask his opinion. Wilson, who knew very little if anything about Connies, also inspected the trouble area and waited to see what would be done about it.

When the inspections had all been completed Toolie fastened the bulkhead door back into place with neat care, aware as he did so that the chances were good that the big bird would never fly again. When he had done this he went up front, sat down at the flight engineer's station, and looked once more at the complex equipment which he knew so well and which had been his life for the past three years. He took out the log and carefully entered the need for maintenance. He added the formal statement that the aircraft was unsafe to fly and signed it off with his name and title.

He took the log book with him when he left the great silent aircraft, called Herb Stallings to one side, and showed him the entry. Without hesitation Stallings added his own name and the numbers which gave him the right to earn his living as a pilot. Toolie returned the log book to its proper place in the rack and then gave some thought to securing the plane against the hurricane winds which were due within a few hours' time. There was little he could do, but for Galloway's sake he wanted to make it good. Also, in his own heart the once proud Super-Constellation had taken the place of much that life had denied him, and he loved her too. He wanted to give her her chance.

He ended by deciding to leave her right where she was. She was on the opposite side of the terminal building from the hangar, which should protect her when the hangar went, regardless of the direction. Since the bird at least looked larger than the building, being in the lee of the structure meant little, but it was the best he had to offer her. He filled the tanks full, adding tons of ballast which would give her a slightly better chance. He checked that the parking brakes were set as firmly as possible. He pushed the wheel chocks tight against the tires and kicked them firmly into position. He thought of sandbagging the wings, but there were no bags available and the labor would have been backbreaking. None of the ramp employees had appeared, not even the usually reliable Armando, who took such pride in his position as an airline representative. When he had finished his work he looked up and saw the first beginnings of daylight. He listened and heard the beat of the surf; it had quickened in the last two hours and the spray was flinging itself a few inches higher toward the sky.

Meanwhile everything which manpower and the fork-lift truck could do to secure the area against the coming fury had been done. The spare engines had been moved into the terminal building and lifted up on blocks against the intrusion of flood water. Some additional equipment, including the office command communications set, had been loaded into the DC-3, which bore the proud name *Santa Isabel* and answered informally to *Lizzie*. The tool crib and spares cage in the hangar had been carefully locked, even though it was an empty gesture. Stallings had another view. "Remember," he told Galloway, "hurricanes have funny ways. Sometimes they go on, sometimes they turn and go back on themselves. You can never be sure. I won't bet on it, but we might come back and find this old box just the way we left her."

Not expressed was the thought that in that case the big Constellation would be sitting proudly waiting for them too.

Toward dawn Galloway went out to the four-engined bird, which didn't understand that it was being abandoned, and climbed on board. He sat for several minutes in the left-hand commander's seat and stared at the instrument panel. He touched the trim tab, the automatic pilot, the communications sets, the nosewheel steering, the oxygen supply, then the propeller controls, the trim tab levers, the cowl flaps controls and all of the intricate mechanism at the flight engineer's station.

He changed his mind and decided to fly her out. Control boost or not he would get her airborne and maneuver her into Miami.

He felt the movement of the airframe when Herb Stallings came on board and walked up the long empty aisle. The big pilot stopped when he reached the cockpit and leaned his huge hands on the back of the two pilot chairs.

"After she has been signed off as unairworthy, it's a violation to try and fly her," he said. "The red tag is on and for a damn good reason. Come." He took Bob Galloway by the hand as he might a small boy and turned him toward the exit.

They walked down the aisle and out the door, which Stallings closed behind him. Without saying anything they crossed the blacktop to the hangar.

Lizzie was almost ready. Toolie was busy checking the last details and making sure that no significant things had been left undone. He borrowed Galloway's keys and secured the terminal building. Then he took down the sign which had been over the door and which bore the emblem of the airline and stowed it on board. "Let's go," he said.

They towed the DC-3 out, heavy with her load and full fuel tanks. Scotty Zimmerman assumed the commander's seat since it was his bird; when Wilson tried to sit down opposite him he motioned the young co-pilot away. "That's for Galloway," he stated. "Go get him."

Bob Galloway sat down on the right-hand seat and looked through the windshield at the long graceful outline of the Connie. *Damn the leak!* She could be replaced, but it wouldn't be Connie. Once more he made the decision to fly her out, and started to rise.

"Don't," Scotty said in one word, and reached up to energize number two. In a few seconds the engine barked into life and the veteran aircraft once more became a living thing. Number one spurted smoke and then cleared up. Lizzie was prepared.

Scotty taxied her slowly to the end of the runway, running through the checklist as he did so. "Passengers secured?" he called back over his shoulder.

"Secured," Wilson reported.

The mag check was fine and the propeller controls responded smoothly during the runup. As practically always, Lizzie had no complaints; she was ready to fly.

Scotty lined up the runway after a careful visual check of

the approach pattern just in case. "Yours," he said to Galloway.

Fighting the dryness in his mouth Bob Galloway put his left hand on the throttles, glanced at the trim tab setting, and took hold of the wheel on the right-hand side. He fed the power in smoothly, lifting the tail up as he firewalled the throttles and put both hands on the wheel. Scotty held the throttles home as Galloway let the fine old bird gather the modest speed she needed to become airborne. Then he eased back and let her come off on her own. He saw the shape of the Connie out of the corner of his eye as he lifted from the ground; then it was past and gone.

"Gear up," he said.

Scotty tuned in the VHF to contact airways control for a clearance. The DC-3 settled down to a steady climb. Below her the whitecaps were thick and full, while far to the left the heavy cumulus could be seen fairly glowering on the horizon.

Chapter Three /

Fifteen hundred feet above the surface of the already rough water of the Caribbean, the turbulent air took free liberties with a small light aircraft which was daring to challenge the elements when they were in a mood of mounting anger. It was painted gray; near the midpoint of the fuselage there was a distinctive triangular decal. As the plane headed toward the southeast both of the men on board kept a close and continuous watch on the constantly shifting pattern of the water below.

In the front seat of the two-place L-6, which bore the proud legend UNITED STATES AIR FORCE, was the pilot, Captain Richard L. Sylvester, CAP. Captain Sylvester, oddly enough, was not in a flight suit; instead he wore the khaki summer class B uniform of the Air Force, complete with a pair of slick wings over his left breast pocket. The wings were slick in that they had no star above to indicate the First Pilot rating (1,500 hours) or the wreath around it to signify the Command Pilot (2,500 hours plus other qualifications). In his personal log book Captain Sylvester could show 610 flight hours since solo, a respectable number doubly distinguished because almost all of them he had paid for out of his own pocket.

He had never been to any military flying school—he had learned the hard way by going out and laying cash on the line for every minute of instruction, on the ground or in the air, that he had ever had. He had made the most of it, and now, in the unfriendly air over the water which was showing its teeth below, he held the little Interstate on course well and corrected the many sudden thrusts of the unstable air with a sure and practiced hand.

The captain's wings varied slightly in pattern from most of the others which the Air Force awards to qualified personnel. Over his right breast pocket he wore a bright red, white and blue patch, which, like everyone else who had one, he detested. It identified him as a member of the Civil Air Patrol, allowed to serve his country without pay, but not to be confused with any of the regular wearers of the Air Force uniform.

In the rear seat was his co-pilot and observer, First Lieutenant Edmund Peter Chang, also in class B uniform, also with the blatant pocket patch, and also with a pair of slick wings which indicated that he was a rated pilot within the CAP requirements. Lieutenant Chang, whose ancestors lay buried somewhere behind the thorny boundaries of Red China, had only 271 hours and was a little worried. All that was keeping his immortal soul inside his body at the moment was the small O-200-5 Franklin engine in the nose of the little plane, which throbbed away, delivering enough of the 102 horsepower which it was rated to keep the aircraft at altitude and on a steady course over the search area. If any one of the four cylinders malfunctioned that would be that, and for all practical purposes the honored ancestors would have their ranks swelled by a new recruit.

Down below, somewhere on the tossing water, there were four men who were in a much worse position. They had been out there for three days in a tiny rubber life raft with little if any water and no food whatever. When the search and rescue requirement had come through, the Civil Air Patrol had responded. The L-6 with the built-in extra-range tanks had been the first to take off; by now it was probably the only one from its base still in the air.

It was still flying, and still headed south, because both Captain Sylvester, at thirty-one years of age, and Lieutenant Chang, at twenty-seven, wanted desperately to find the four imperiled men, or whatever number of them still survived, before the hurricane took over with its reign of violence and sure death. The Air Rescue Service would be out with its own search planes, but ARS could not cover the whole area completely, as witness the fact that since they had left the coastline neither of the flyers had even caught a glimpse of any other aircraft.

The L-6 could fly low and slow, and that was what was needed for an operation like this.

Dick Sylvester tried again to use the small panel radio; he turned it on and was rewarded in a few seconds with a crash of static which drowned out whatever else might have been on the frequency. More sophisticated equipment might have put him through, but the CAP could not afford it and the little tubing-and-fabric aircraft could not have carried it along with the extra gas it needed to survive.

"What do you think, Ed?" he shouted back over the pounding of the engine.

Chang studied the folded chart on his lap once more, read the gas gauges, and consulted the E6B computer which was his other navigational aid.

"Go juice we've got." He leaned forward to make himself better understood. "We can spend another half hour on this heading if you want to."

Sylvester took his eyes off the instrument panel, such as it was, and scanned the water below for a moment. "Pretty strong wind building up," he advised over his shoulder.

"I know it. I figure that increases the probability of the raft being down this way. Want to risk it?"

"How about you?"

"I'm for trying."

"O.K., then." He resumed giving his full attention to piloting the plane and studying the endless, unrewarding water below; on its surface somewhere, God willing, there would be a little blob of orange and the chance to make the whole, somewhat dangerous mission gloriously successful.

A particularly savage gust, resentful of the decision, kicked the left wing high and almost flung the light plane onto its back. Sylvester swung the stick hard to the left and slightly forward to correct the nose-up attitude. The plane came back level and the little engine continued to whirl the single propeller in steady defiance of the colossal forces which were gathering in the sky.

In the rear seat Ed Chang was having second thoughts.

Strangely, they were not of himself, but of his partner; he had more or less forced Sylvester to go on and now he wondered sharply if he had been wise in doing so.

He remembered the men below; the CAP plane might be their last chance for life. In rescue work you don't think of yourself first; that wasn't the idea. He tightened the seat belt across his notably skinny lap and once more focused all of his visual power onto the water blow.

He saw nothing but dirty blue-gray tossing waves and angry whitecaps. If any people were still alive in that rubber life raft, they would have to be deathly seasick. Chang himself was not feeling too well, but he willed his stomach to be quiet while he got on with the job.

Sylvester turned his head and shouted back. "Land! I've got an island up ahead."

Chang looked, but he could not see past the pilot's shoulders. Forward visibility from the rear seat was close to nil. He took the chart in both hands and studied his course line with intense concentration.

"How big?" he asked over the noise in the cabin.

For answer Sylvester turned the little plane thirty degrees so that his partner could see the landfall out the side window. Chang looked, and returned to his chart.

There was no island within sight of where he calculated their position to be, nothing which would be in visible range at this altitude.

But the island was there and it would positively be on the chart.

When he found what it might be, there was a sudden tightening of his stomach muscles with the alarming discovery of their probable true position. Before he reported he turned his E6B computer onto its back and carefully adjusted the scales. Then he leaned forward and tried to make his voice loud and calm at the same time.

"Brace yourself. If that little key is what I think it is, then we've got a tailwind quartering of almost sixty knots."

"Say again," Sylvester shouted.

"Sixty knots—no wonder it's rough."

"Can we get back?"

Chang drew a deep breath. "With this wind, and our known position, it's close. If this wind gains any more, we could buy the farm."

It was the cold hard truth, but it was a time for facing facts.

Dick Sylvester felt a lump in his gullet. He had the responsibility as aircraft commander. It might be a ridiculously little cheap aircraft built back in 1943, but he had his own butt in it and it was his command.

He responded as the A/C of a B-52H intercontinental eight-engined jet bomber might have done. "What are the alternates?" he shouted.

Chang had anticipated the question and was studying the chart again. He made his decision as an officer would be expected to do, and reported. "Best bet is Tres Santos. It's the nearest airport and more or less dead ahead. We can search on the way; plenty of gas to get there."

"What's it got, anything?"

"Yes—fuel, maintenance, lights, five-thousand-foot paved runway."

"Hangar?"

"Must have. Take us about an hour to get there."

By this time they had flown past the tiny island which had

given them their fix and could see nothing but open water ahead.

"Your recommendation?" That was the right question to put to a navigator.

"Affirmative."

Sylvester made his decision. "Give me a heading."

"One six niner."

"One six niner, wilco."

The craft lifted the right wing slightly, hit a bump, straightened out, and assumed its new course. Despite its limitations, it gave nothing to any other plane in the sky. It was low, slow, inefficient, more or less obsolete, unsophisticated, single-engined, laughably small, crude of structure, and proud. It flew the same airways as the great jets, it carried the name of the United States Air Force, and it was infinitely superior, in its own opinion, to the millions upon millions of earthbound vehicles which were permanently wedded to the paved highways and which could not cross a shoreline until somebody built a bridge. The little fixed-pitch propeller continued to slash at the air, the fabric-covered wings endured the bumps and jolts, and the engine kept up the steady rhythm which meant life and survival to the two men inside.

It had no de-icers, very limited radio, no ILS, no DME, no heated windshield, no propeller alcohol, no pressurization, no retractable landing gear, no radar—nothing to help it but the few primary instruments and an artificial horizon driven by a four-inch ventura tube, which, in a real storm, could ice up quickly and rob the only gyro on board of its power to show the attitude.

But it knew its business and by heaven it could fly.

Captain Sylvester held it on course well, considering the turbulence, and kept his eye on his watch as well as on the water below. After forty-five minutes he added power and began to climb at a rate of four hundred feet per minute. Six minutes later he leveled off at four thousand feet and looked ahead for any sign of land that might herald Tres Santos airport.

Lieutenant Chang was a good navigator within his resources—at fifty-six minutes after altering course Sylvester spotted a spit of land and shortly thereafter the surface of the runway. He turned on the radio and prepared to call the tower.

"Frequency?" he shouted.

Chang supplied it. Sylvester tuned the set, picked up the mike and gave his call.

"Tres Santos, Tres Santos, this is CAP 667 in sight north of the field. Request landing instructions."

There was no answer.

Sylvester guided the aircraft into the normal traffic pattern and repeated the call, again without result. He then tuned to the international distress frequency, 121.5, and gave it one more try.

When he did not get an answer for the third time, he was careful to follow the book. "Tres Santos, this is CAP 667. I am declaring an emergency due to low fuel supply and am making an emergency landing your field. Turning base leg."

Despite the heavy, buffeting winds he guided the small craft into an acceptable pattern after carefully checking visually for any other traffic and estimating the surface wind. Once pointed toward the runway he concentrated on his final approach. The runway was far longer than he would need, but the crosswind was making itself felt and at the slow rate of approach of the L-6 it was accentuated.

He came over the numbers well, in good attitude and ready to flare. As he started to lower the tail the crosswind set up a drift angle he could not accept; he pushed the stick forward and went for a wheels-on landing instead. When he bumped the tires cleanly onto the concrete, he felt a great sense of relief surge through him to be back on the ground after the long and trying flight. Because the runway was reasonably wide he deliberately turned a few degrees to cut down the crosswind component. It was a good idea, but a savage gust caught the Interstate just below control speed; she was helpless and weathercocked.

Sylvester looked ahead quickly and saw hard scrub grass along the left side of the runway. That was all right; he could run off there with no danger. He kept the tail up in case of ditches, but found none—instead directly before him he saw a small block of some sort on which was mounted a runway light. He had no choice but to straddle it. He felt the sharp spat as the tip of the propeller hit it; then they were past, the tail settled down and the light plane rolled to a stop.

Now headed more or less into the wind, Sylvester taxied his plane directly up to the terminal behind the big four-engined Super-Constellation which was on the ramp. He knew better than to leave a small aircraft behind an airliner that could blow it to pieces with one of its engines so he kept steadily on until he was right before the doorway and to some extent, at least, in the lee of the building.

He cut the engine, and let relative quiet settle around him.

"Wow," he said with exhaling breath. He made no apology for running off the runway; Chang knew what had happened. In the time between the loss of flying speed and the moment when the tail is securely on the ground a plane of that type would be for a few seconds almost impossible to control under heavy crosswind conditions.

"We're here, if not with dignity," Chang said.

"Any landing you walk away from is a good landing. Let's tie Betsy down and check in."

Stiff from hours of confinement in a set, close position, the two pilots climbed out and surveyed the situation. There seemed to be no one on the ramp; the hangar doors were closed. There was no visible place where light planes were to be parked and no tie-down facilities could be seen.

"Tie her now to one of those posts in front of the terminal," the captain directed. "I'll go inside and see if we can make it back; if not I'll find out where we should put her."

He walked briskly up to the door, still ashamed of the fact that he had messed up the landing because of the crosswind. If he got out of it at the price of a few cracks he was lucky— he might have to pay for a runway light globe.

The door to the terminal was locked. Sylvester walked carefully around the small building and tried the three other doors; none would admit him. In a way it was a relief because of the landing, in a way foreboding. He walked to the hangar and tried it. Locked. There was a small external tower and he could see from the ground there was no one in it. To be sure he walked over and tried the door; it too was locked. He went back to the plane.

"We're alone," he announced.

"We've got to close our flight plan," Chang reminded him. "If we don't they'll be out in force looking for *us*."

"Everything seems to be locked up. We may have to wait

until the Connie crew gets here. It may be five minutes, but it could be two or three hours."

"Let's take another look," Chang suggested. With the tail of the plane securely tied to a concrete post they went together and explored every door and window; without exception they were locked.

Sylvester rubbed his head. "We can do one of two things: we can just sit it out and wait for the Connie crew, or we can bust a window and break in. I don't like to do that, but we are past our arrival time now and the flight plan is still open."

"Let's wait fifteen minutes," his co-pilot proposed. "If the Connie crew isn't here by that time, or if no one shows up, then I vote we break in." He looked at his watch. "It's close to noon and they may go to lunch early here. That will give us ten minutes to get through to close our flight plan before they start emergency procedures."

"I saw a phone on the desk in there," the captain said. "All right, we'll wait fifteen minutes."

After nearly twenty anxious, impatient minutes, Edmund Chang picked up a good-sized stone. "I've decided where to do it," he announced. "The small window on the right side, the one higher up. It's probably the head, which means if water gets in there shouldn't be any damage to speak of."

Sylvester nodded. "Good thinking. I don't like to do it, but there'll be worse trouble if we don't report in."

Chang broke the window neatly with the rock, reached through to release the catch, and slid it open. He wiggled his thin form through the opening and a few moments later opened the front door from the inside.

"Welcome," he said.

Captain Sylvester lost no time heading for the office where he had noted the phone through the window. This time the door was not locked. He seated himself behind the desk and picked up the instrument. Chang flopped himself onto the two-place chrome-and-plastic settee.

Sylvester listened and jiggled the button. Then he spun the dial to OPERATOR, listened, and waited. He tried it again, carefully, and then looked up.

"The line's dead," he said.

Chapter Four /

ED CHANG SAT SILENTLY. HE REASONED THAT it was a good time to keep his mouth shut.

Dick Sylvester wiped his sleeve across his forehead. "There are several things we can do now," he said, after he had his thoughts in order. "We can wait a reasonable time for them to get the telephone line back in commission."

"I wouldn't bet too much on that. With this storm coming on, it could take two or three days."

"We could start down the road and see what we find."

"And miss the Connie crew," Chang added.

"Of course, you're right," Sylvester agreed. "Then let's see if we can find some eighty-octane gas, fill Betsy up, and fly back. We'll need close to forty gallons. If I leave twenty bucks on the desk with a note and my home address, that ought to take care of it, and the window. We can continue the search on the way."

"No good," Chang said. "I didn't want to tell you this right away, but when you hit that landing light you broke the prop tip. It's not serious, the engine's O.K., but as it is Betsy can't fly."

"Under emergency conditions it might be all right."

Ed Chang shook his head. "The prop is out of balance; after half an hour she'd shake the crankshaft right out of the engine. You know that."

Dick Sylvester did know it, as he also knew that an emergency repair was out of the question.

"Then we wait for the Connie crew and that's all we can do."

Chang got up. "That's the way I see it. Considering the way the weather is worsening, they can't be too much longer."

Sylvester sat silently a moment in thought. "Listen," he said finally, "we can't fly Betsy and the hangar is locked. Furthermore, what do you think are the chances of that hangar surviving a hurricane more or less head-on?"

Ed walked over and studied the structure through the window. "Not too good," he admitted.

"Now, when the Connie boys get here, they aren't going to wait around very long. If they are headed stateside we might be able to get them to take us along. If not, then we're in trouble. But in any event what about Betsy?"

"I'm listening," Chang said.

"I think we ought to bring her in here."

The lieutenant let surprise show in his face. "How?" he asked.

"We can take the wings off and roll her in through the cargo-room door. We'll probably have to pay storage charges, but we can't leave her out there. She wouldn't have a chance, no matter how we tie her down."

"To take the wings off we need tools. Any around here would be in the hangar and that's pretty well secured."

"I thought of that," the captain said. "But I know where the necessary tools are and it shouldn't be too difficult."

"Tell me," Chang said.

"On the Connie, probably in the flight engineer's gear."

Chang hesitated. "You know," he confessed, "I don't mind breaking a window in an emergency situation we can prove, but it's another matter to go on board an airliner like that and start meddling with the gear. The A/C or the engineer could get mighty sore about that and those guys are our best bet for getting out of here."

"Then I'll do it. If the crew comes while we're working, I'll apologize and explain immediately. If we finish before they do, we can put the tools back where we found them and nobody will be hurt."

Chang deliberated. "I'm still squeamish about going on board the Connie. Interfering or meddling with an airliner is a serious thing. But since it's Betsy's only chance, for her I'll do it."

"Then let's get going," Sylvester said. "It's my idea so I'll go get the tools."

He walked outside facing the stiff wind and climbed up the long flight of steps to the rear cabin door. He seized the handle with both hands, rotated it, and felt the latches release. He slid the door aside and stepped on board.

The rows of seats in the rear cabin rebuked him silently for the intrusion. He walked up the aisle, with the feeling that he was entering the wrong church during services, and opened the door in the forward bulkhead. Ahead of him there yawned a long, functional cargo hold with a bare metal floor and load markings painted on the sides. He had not realized how huge the Super-Connie was until he saw it now, an unwilling host to his presence.

He steeled himself a little as he made his way through the freight section on up to the flight deck. He paused there and looked for a moment at the great complexity of instruments, levers, and controls. They were on all sides and overhead; every bit of space not needed for the windshield was crammed with gear. He remembered his errand and began to search for the tool kit; presently he found it against a bulkhead next to the crew latrine. His luck held: there was no padlock fastening the lid shut as he had feared there might be. He raised the cover and there before him was a clean set of the most useful aircraft tools. He selected two sturdy screwdrivers, one regular and one Phillips, an assortment of wrenches, and two sizes of pliers—one with a cutter which could be used to extract cotter keys. With his find he hurried back down the long length of the Constellation and out the door, which he carefully shut behind him.

Neither he nor Chang had ever taken the wings off an aircraft before, but it was not too difficult a job. They removed the fairing first at the wing root, then they uncoupled the gas lines leading from the wing tanks and the electrical connection to the navigation light in the wingtip. After that it was a matter of three bolts, two at the wing fittings and one where the bracing strut joined the fuselage.

Chang did the final bolt removals while Sylvester kept the wingtip from falling. "Be careful," the lieutenant advised.

"If we break or distort any of these fittings, we've really had it."

The wing came off cleanly and together they lowered it to the ground. It was amazingly light, but hard to handle in the stiff wind. Together they managed to manhandle it against the dynamic forces into the terminal cargo section. When they had finished, they were sweating.

"One more," Sylvester said, and they went back.

Now the little plane was leaning crazily on one wheel, her remaining wingtip resting on the ground. They tipped her back up and removed the other wing somewhat more easily, having learned how. In fifteen minutes they had the second wing stowed, and returned for the final time to get the fuselage.

Stripped of the wings without which she was all but helpless the plane looked strangely naked and rejected. They pulled her by the tail through the roll-up cargo door and into the sanctuary of the cargo room. As soon as they were finished Sylvester took the tools and, restraining the impulse to run, returned them to the kit from which they had been taken. When he had closed the aircraft's door behind him for the second time he felt a definite sense of relief.

Chang secured the cargo door to the terminal and asked, "Have you seen anything to eat around here?" Together they searched the modest premises, but there was not even a coffee maker.

It was now ten minutes after one, almost an hour and a half past the time when they should have reported themselves safe on the ground. Search procedures would now be under way, expensive procedures which would also involve some element of risk for those concerned. Single-engine flights over water, as a steady thing, are not compatible with longevity. They both knew it well.

"I'm going to take a look, just in case the crew is coming or someone is in the pattern," Sylvester said. Now that he had done as much as he could the inaction chafed him and he was sharply worried that he had been unable to close out his flight plan. He strode to the field door of the terminal, jerked it open, and felt his heart freeze.

A man was standing on the other side.

He was tall and broad, and looked even larger because of the oversize, ragged straw hat he wore. His heavy, sunburned features branded him a Latin-American, the ragged shirt and catch-as-catch-can trousers put him unmistakably in the category of a manual laborer. He wore crude leather sandals on his otherwise bare feet. The fierceness in his face was largely due to a massive mustache which gave him almost a Mongolian cast. He looked as though he could raise his hardened hands and break Sylvester in two with a single effort.

The captain's voice jammed in his throat; for the first time in his life he was completely and utterly frightened.

"*Americano capitan,*" the man said in a raspy baritone; then he turned and walked away.

Sylvester partly recovered himself. "Ed!" he called urgently.

Chang, who was in the latrine, did not respond at once. When he did come, the man was already out of sight behind the hangar and Sylvester was not entirely sure that his senses had not played him a particularly violent trick. He told what had happened quickly to his co-pilot, who also wondered if Sylvester really had seen someone. But hallucinations do not ordinarily come in broad daylight, with the sun close to the zenith of the sky.

"Either you scared him worse than he scared you, or he'll be back," Chang said. "Maybe he had a little polite thievery in mind and you frightened him off."

By one-thirty there had been no sign of the Connie crew, no other aircraft had appeared near the field, and even the frightening intruder had not returned. "In a sense we're trapped," Sylvester said. "We can't go anywhere or we might miss the crew, we can't fly our own aircraft, we can't phone and, outside of my friend, no one knows we are here."

"I can start teaching you Chinese," Chang suggested. "Or how about karate, the manly art of self-defense?"

"That might be more to the point."

Chang walked over and looked out the window. "The mystery is about to be solved," he announced. "We have company on the way."

The company coming up the road consisted of the man whom Sylvester had seen followed by a shapeless woman in misfitting garments; between them they were carrying something not clearly visible. In the heat and brightness of the near-noonday they appeared more ragged than terrifying.

They came through the open door as a procession, the man in front, the woman behind, their burden in the middle. It was a crude litter and on it there was a young adult male who tried to turn as he was set down in the middle of the floor. He, too, was clearly a Latin with about two days' accumulation of beard. "Allo," he said.

Chang dropped onto one knee beside him. "Speak English, fellow?" he asked.

"Sí, Chino," the man on the litter said. "Not too good, but some."

"What's the matter?"

"I got big pain in my belly. You understand Spanish?"

"No hablo español," Chang replied.

Sylvester, ignoring the older man and woman, was standing by, listening.

"I am Armando," the patient said. "I work this airport. Work for Señor Galloway."

"Do you know when the Connie crew is due here?" Sylvester asked.

The question was ignored. "Yesterday I get pain in belly. It get bigger so I no come to work, understand?"

"*Sí*," Chang answered.

"I think I know what I got, but can't say in English."

Sylvester took charge. "Let me try something," he said. Kneeling down he gently probed the abdomen of the man on the litter; at a point one third of the way from the navel to the hipbone he found the most sensitive spot. "I'd guess appendicitis," he said professionally, "but I'm not a doctor. I think you should see one right away; a surgeon might be better. Those things can't wait too long."

"*Sí*, I know. There is no doctor. One doctor, he go away."

"Ouch," Chang interjected.

Sylvester looked up at the man and the woman, standing silently watching them. He guessed correctly that the language barrier was between them, and that because of it they were letting the younger man do the necessary talking.

"We are not doctors," Sylvester said slowly. "We are pilots. We landed here a couple of hours ago."

Armando clenched his teeth for a moment, then relaxed his jaw and spoke again. "I know," he said. "My father," he nodded toward the older man, "he see you."

"Listen, Armando," Sylvester said slowly, "our aircraft is broken; it cannot fly. Otherwise we would take you out of here to a doctor, do you understand?"

"I do," Armando said.

Sylvester went on: "Our airplane is very small and very slow. It would be a very rough ride and you would be in great pain. Understand?"

"Sí, yes."

"There is a Constellation here ready to go out, the big airliner. It can take you to a doctor much faster. I know they will take you. I promise you they will. Is that clear?"

Armando rolled his head from side to side.

"I know this Connie very well," he said. "It is Señor Galloway's. This morning he go away in the Goonie. He not come back until after storm pass. You understand?"

"Yes, but then he will send a crew for the Constellation. He can't leave it here; the storm would break it. They will come soon; they must."

Again the young man rolled his head as though the bone segments within his neck had separated.

"He no send crew. Connie crew was here. Señor Stallings, I know him. They go out with Señor Galloway in the Goonie. They not come back now."

"That's impossible," Ed Chang said.

Sylvester nodded to the man on the litter and got to his feet. "Back in a minute. Come over here a minute, Ed, I want to talk to you." He almost put the force of a command into his words.

Sylvester and Chang walked to the other end of the terminal waiting area and stopped there.

"Can you buy that?" the captain asked.

"Possibly, it depends."

"On what?"

"Well, for one thing suppose the Connie has a mechanical. Something so bad that she can't be flown."

41

Sylvester shook his head. "It doesn't fit. In that case they would have put her in the hangar to give her some protection at least. Not out on the line where she is now."

"There's one way we can tell; we can check the tanks. If she's down for maintenance, they wouldn't have topped her off. If she's full, then that's not the answer."

"I think she's full. She's pretty well down on the shock struts and the cargo hold is empty."

"Assuming she's full, what other explanation is there?"

Captain Sylvester thought about that one a long time. He walked up and down a few paces and looked out the window. "I've got one idea," he said finally.

"I'd like to hear it."

"Do you remember the time, not so long ago, when the FAA deliberately crashed a DC-7 out in the desert to find out how it broke up?"

"I do. It damn near killed me at the time." Lieutenant Chang shook his head. "A big, beautiful DC-7, probably not five years old."

"Right."

Now it was Chang's turn to think. "You have the idea that the Connie was deliberately spotted out on the ramp, right in the path of the storm, for a *test?* Just to see how badly she'd get smashed up?"

"They did it to a DC-7—that's an even later model, and faster."

"An engine *could* be out," Chang persisted.

"A Connie flies fine on three engines; it can on two. I've read about it. In an emergency like this, they could take her out on three fans."

"Particularly empty," he added as an afterthought.

"Think hard. Is there any other answer?"

Dick Sylvester did think hard. He thought until he could almost feel the effort within his skull. "I can't come up with anything else," he confessed at last. "She can't be abandoned for the insurance, that's impossible. With the crew right here this morning the underwriters would never buy it."

"Agreed, I thought of that too."

"Then it narrows down to this: either Armando is all wet and the crew is on its way in now, or else the Connie has been deliberately staked out for some kind of sadistic test."

"Or an engine is out, the gear won't come up, or something like that. It hasn't been completely eliminated."

"We fly Betsy with the gear down; it's welded that way. It would have to be a helluva mechanical to abandon a fully-equipped, four-engine Super-Constellation without even shoving it into the hangar. Those things will fly under a lot of adverse conditions. If the tanks are full, that ought to give us the answer."

Chang saw the logic of that and had to agree. "Let's talk to Armando some more," he suggested. "So far we have only his word to go on."

They went back to the three people who were patiently waiting for their return. Dick Sylvester knelt down beside the litter. "Armando, how do you feel?" he asked.

"Not so good," the young man confessed. "I need doctor."

"We know that," Sylvester said. "The first plane that comes in we'll ask to help you, no matter who's flying it."

Again Armando rolled his head in the hopeless manner he had used before. "Nobody come," he insisted. "Everybody go Miami. Just light this morning they go. Señor Galloway, Señor Stallings, black man. Everybody they go. My father he coming to airport when he see them go. Why they no take Connie I not know."

"That's twice he's used those same names," Chang pointed out. "Do you know any of the Connie crews?" he asked.

"Sí, I know them all. I work here. I put in gas. I do many things. I know them all. They all go away."

"Do you know who flies the Connie?" the captain asked. "Do you know who the flight engineer is?"

The patient fought against his pain and the mounting attempt to make himself believed. "I tell you, Señor Stallings, Capitan Stallings, he fly Connie. Black man, Sims, is engineer. He go away too, I know. I not fool."

"Blackman Sims," Chang repeated, "I don't think he could dream up a name like that."

"Not in this country anyway," Sylvester answered. "All right, what next?"

For answer the older man came over and mutely spread his hands in supplication. It was more eloquent than any speech could have been.

"He wants us to look after his boy," Sylvester said. "I'm with him. But we aren't doctors. If we tried any emergency surgery we'd kill him. Besides, we don't have anything to work with. I don't even have a pocket knife, do you?"

"No," Chang answered.

Armando spoke. "I know you not doctor. But you United States Air Force, capitan and lieutenant, I know. My father, my mother bring me here. You save my life. You fly me stateside to doctor."

Sylvester looked up quickly. "How bad is that prop?" he asked.

"Three inches broken from the end."

That tore it.

"Please we go," Armando pleaded. "You fly me stateside now in Connie?"

Chapter Five

ED CHANG REACHED DOWN AND TOOK THE man's hand in his own. "You don't understand," he said, his voice a little thick. "We're not Connie pilots. We fly only little light airplanes, one engine. It takes months to learn to fly an airliner like the Connie. We don't know how."

With his other hand Armando reached up and touched the wings pinned to the slender lieutenant's chest. "United States Air Force," he said. "You fly anything."

Chang looked up toward his partner; he raised his head slowly and there was a fresh intensity in his narrow eyes. "Let's go outside and look at the bird," he said.

Sylvester understood. "We'll be right back," he promised. Together the captain and the lieutenant went out and looked at the huge Constellation which stood there silently, waiting.

"We can't do it, Ed," Sylvester said. "I know how much is at stake, but we can't stick our necks out that far, and risk all of the legal complications involved, just on Armando's say-so that no crew is coming. He wants a ride and he wants it badly—I think he'd say anything to get it."

Chang went to the passenger steps and released the lock. "Before I say anything, I want to find out for sure if she's gassed. That will answer a lot of questions—I want to know."

He rolled the steps against the wing close to the fuselage, climbed up, and stepped carefully over onto the aluminum surface. When he reached the first of the gas intake ports he carefully removed the cover plate and the heavy cap underneath, and looked inside. Then he replaced the cap and plate as they had been, walked somewhat gingerly to the outboard gas-loading station, and repeated the process. Without saying anything he came back to the loading steps and climbed down. "She's full," he reported.

"How about the other side?"

"It has to be the same. How much gas would you say she held altogether?"

"Maybe four thousand gallons," Sylvester guessed.

"All right, at six pounds per gallon that's twelve tons of gas in her wings. Put six on one side, particularly out toward the end and how would she sit?"

"Lopsided," the captain agreed. "We know she's full, what next?"

"I'm satisfied now she's on the line ready to go," Chang said carefully. "So, Armando or not, I'm waiting for the crew to come and get her."

Together they rolled the steps back to the loading door and carefully locked them into position.

"The wind is still rising," Sylvester said. "Did you take a

look at that spray breaking against the rock over there?"

Chang paused, and listened to the sound and sweep of the wind.

"It's getting too rough for Betsy," he answered. "I'm glad she's safe inside." He looked at the leaning palm trees by the terminal and shook his head. "They can't be much longer," he added. "Not even a Connie can take off in a gale."

Sylvester gripped his arm. "You're right! Look."

A vehicle was coming down the road, at a good speed, toward the terminal.

They watched it intently as it approached, dust in its wake, clearly intent on making what speed it could over the far from perfect surface of the highway.

"And that's that," Chang said, relief choking his voice. "It had me going for a while."

The vehicle, an ancient Chevrolet of indefinite color, reached the entrance, turned in and came directly out onto the ramp. It had barely stopped when the driver stepped out—a very tall man who towered at least six feet four and who looked all the taller for the plain black clerical cassock which he wore from chin to ankle. He was elderly, but not old—his face a fine web of countless lines engraved in the flesh, branded there by weather, age, the relentlessness of the sun, and possibly also by the trials which went with his calling. "I'm so glad I arrived before you departed," he said in careful, stilted English. "I am Father Ferrara."

Dick Sylvester hid his sharp disappointment and shook hands briefly. "I'm Captain Sylvester; this is Lieutenant Chang. We were on a search and rescue mission this morning and had to land here."

"I know of your landing," the priest said. "I saw you come in."

"It may be a good thing you are here, Father," Ed Chang

interjected. "There is a man inside who is seriously ill and may need your help. Can you get him a doctor?"

"I am afraid you must do that; we have no doctor here. We had one, but he is gone. We do not even have a midwife, and we have need of one. But that is not all."

"What is it, Father?" Sylvester asked.

The tall priest motioned toward the ancient car. "I have a little girl of eight years here; she is burned. It happened only a little while ago. The high wind blew fire and it caught her clothing."

"Oh, no!" Chang said. The lines about his mouth tightened. He opened and closed his hands as though they were anxious to do something, but had no employment.

"A few months ago a U.S. Navy doctor gave me a first-aid kit," the priest went on. "In it I found a tube with a morphine needle. I have given it to her and she sleeps. But it will not be for too long and she must see a doctor."

"Father, have you a telephone, a radio, anything to send for one?" Sylvester asked. Hope and anxiety mixed in his voice.

"Our phones are not working. There is one here, but I am sure you cannot use it. I knew you would fly Armando to the States in the big airplane. I ask now for the sake of mercy you take this little girl too. That is why I came so fast, to reach you before you departed."

Ed Chang seized the conversation. "Father, do you know anything about the crew of this airplane? Where are they? When will they return?"

"They have gone, very early this morning in one of the smaller planes. Right after my prayers I was coming to ask them to take care of my people before the storm, but they left suddenly just after daylight. I know most of them and one, Señor Wilson, comes to my church when he is here on Sunday. All are gone."

"But they must be coming back!"

The priest spread his hands. "Is it logical they would leave here then? Why depart when they have already arrived!"

"Yet they left the Connie."

The priest's smile waned, a touch of impatience in his features. "I do not understand all these things. But they were here and they have gone, this I can tell you."

Dick Sylvester looked again toward the shoreline and the foaming surf which thundered relentlessly against the retaining rocks. "Father, you said you saw this plane come in last night. Did you mean that literally? You actually saw it with your own eyes?"

"Yes, of course. I was visiting the little community here— there is one for the people who work here at the airport and their families. It is not far away. I myself saw the plane come in. I have seen it many times. It is so beautiful in the air—the most beautiful of airplanes when it flies."

"Now please think carefully, Father. Were all four engines running, can you be sure of that? Did it sound any different than it usually does? Was anything at all different about it?"

The priest, his face set, shook his head. "A little lower, perhaps because of the wind, but all engines were running, I am sure of that." He stretched himself to his full height and towered over his two interrogators. "Much time which God will not return to our hands is being lost," he said, a firmness in his voice. "Armando cannot wait, the morphine will not last forever. When Armando was so sick last night I was called. We prayed that we should receive help. We were heard, as we are always heard, and we were answered. You came, two pilots in your small airplane."

At that moment Dick Sylvester would have sold his soul to have gone to a flying school where he would have been taught instruments, multi-engine flying, where he would have been prepared to assume command of a Super-Constellation in flight. His entire training had consisted of brief ground school, ten hours of dual instruction, and a few scattered flight checks after that, from which he had learned little if anything. He had earned his wings honorably; he had paid every penny of his training expenses and had rented the airplanes in which he had logged the six hundred plus hours which he had. He had laid out more to belong to the Civil Air Patrol, to buy his uniforms, to attend the meetings, to fly whenever he had the chance. For all this he was paid nothing—he was not even given any flight training to improve his skills.

Before him the great Constellation bulked against the sky.

"To be the answer to someone's prayer would be the greatest thing in my life, Father." He spoke quietly, bitterly ashamed of his own inadequacy. The incessant wind clawed at his face and found unmanly moisture in the corner of his eyes; he turned his face to hide his disgrace.

"We have never flown a Constellation," Ed Chang said, very simply.

The priest was unshaken. "God will guide you. I will bless you and your mission."

"We have no authority to take this plane. We could go to prison."

"Never." The priest once more drew himself fully erect. "If you are ever accused I myself will come and tell them what you did for us in answer to our need. They will believe me. They will respect my word."

Dick Sylvester pressed his lips together without speaking.

He walked away from the two of them, to be alone. He walked under the wing of the great aircraft and looked up at the powerful engines jutting out from the wing in their nacelles. He walked over and laid his hand on the massive tire closest to him on the main landing gear. He walked out and surveyed the long sweep of forward fuselage and the radar-tipped nose of the great craft. He felt the tons upon tons of its bulk pressing down above him and saw the vast reach of its wings.

He rested both hands on the other main gear and bowed his head.

"God, help me to do it," he said silently.

Captain Richard Lloyd Sylvester of the Civil Air Patrol, an auxiliary of the United States Air Force, responded as he knew an officer and a gentleman should. He straightened and walked back to the others.

He did not have to speak; Chang already knew.

"You go on board and start familiarizing yourself with the cockpit," Chang said quietly. "I'll take charge of loading the patients."

The decision made, Captain Sylvester climbed the steps rapidly to the door, opened it with assurance, and started down the aisle to the cockpit. When he reached it he sat down in the left-hand commander's seat and adjusted the belt. Then he experimented with the levers underneath the chair until he found how they operated; he moved forward and up some until he felt that the position was comfortable for him. He took hold of the wheel and put his feet on the rudder pedals. That helped him a little—for all of its size the Connie was still an airplane and he knew that once it was airborne he could at least keep her straight and level.

He had never flown a wheel-controlled airplane, but he

knew how it was to be done and that the change-over was easy. He began to read the signs which some wonderfully inspired genius of an engineer had placed next to the most of the controls. He located the nosewheel steering at his left knee and fitted his hand experimentally over the small wheel at the top of the shaft. There would be a power boost on that—if he knew how to turn it on. Perhaps it was automatic. He fitted his right hand across the span of the four throttles in the center pedestal and looked out the windshield.

You poured the coal to all four engines and released the brakes. There was no doubt of that. Then you let her gain speed until you could feel her grip the air. Then you lifted off the nosewheel a little way and let her come off on her own. That would be it. After that she was an L-6 with four engines and so what? At least he would play it that way—it was the only way he knew.

First Lieutenant Edmund Peter Chang, United States Air Force, Civil Air Patrol, was ready—his uniform was an obligation and he would not fail it. In as professional a manner as he could muster he returned to the terminal and informed Armando, and through him his anxious parents, that the plane was about to leave. He did not waste time pointing out the grave uncertainties of the trip; it could do no good and much harm. With Father Ferrara to help him he took the front of the litter and carried the stricken man out to the aircraft. With the priest holding his end high, they took it up the boarding steps and maneuvered it into the cabin.

It was the first time Chang had been on board and he looked quickly around. "Let's take him up forward." He nodded toward the bulkhead. "There may be a lounge or something in the first-class section."

They crossed into the cargo hold and were disillusioned. Chang re-evaluated the situation and then directed that the litter be placed across the foremost row of seats in the rear cabin. "It will keep him off the floor if it gets drafty," he explained.

While he secured the litter with straps he found in the cargo hold, the priest disappeared to return with a sleeping child, wrapped in a blanket, in his arms. Chang quickly pulled out the dividers in a bank of three seats so that she would have an impromptu bed. Then he fastened her as gently as possible in position with two of the seat belts. His lips moved silently as he worked.

When he had finished, he went forward and reported. "The passengers are secured. The Father is still on board—he can look after them while we figure out how to get this bird started."

Captain Sylvester nodded. "Fine. I think you will have to man the flight engineer's station for the take-off; from the look of things the engines are started from over there. After we get going, then you better come up here and help me fly."

"Right, captain." He hadn't meant to overdo it that way; it was a false note.

"Ed," Sylvester said seriously, "let's face the facts. I give us a fifty percent chance, or perhaps a little better than that, to get out of this alive and in one piece. We're going to need all the brains, luck, and knowledge that we both have combined to have any chance at all. So we can't stand on ceremony. Understand?"

Chang looked at him. "I know that, Dick. But let's fly our colors while we can. We may need them before we're through."

Sylvester swung around in the captain's chair. "Ed," he said, and held out his hand. Silently they shook hands, as a bond of mutual trust, and at least a measure of prayer.

Sylvester turned back and once more surveyed the maze of instruments, warning lights, radio controls, switches, throttles, propeller pitch levers, the autopilot, the fire control system, the engine cut-off valves, the ILS and DME equipment, the radar scope, the de-icing gear, the overhead panel, which was crammed with toggles for the lighting systems, warning horns, and all of the other intricate complexities which made up the cockpit of the four-engined Lockheed airliner.

He located the three trimming controls, the magnetic compass, the sensitive altimeter, and the instrument which had replaced the artificial horizon with which he was familiar. He carefully set the altimeter for ten feet above sea level and read the barometric pressure which showed in the window. It was 28.84; the hurricane was closer than he had thought and for a moment he felt a touch of panic. He fought it down and forced himself to finger each of the controls so that at least the feel would be familiar.

While he was doing this, Ed Chang sat at the flight engineer's station looking up at the hopeless complexity of the master control panel. In a few minutes he would have to operate it; the thought came to him that probably they wouldn't even be able to start the engines. Now they had gone this far, he did not want to fail for that absurd reason. He didn't want to see a man die, and a child suffer in agony, because he didn't know how to start a piston engine. If they got one going, then the other three should be easier. With the engines running, then pound for pound they would probably have more power than Betsy could boast. Also he felt that Dick Sylvester was a better pilot than he himself realized. At least he hoped so.

"You know what, Ed," Sylvester said in the quiet of the cockpit. "There's one thing I'd certainly like to do."

"What's that?"

"Read the directions."

Something snapped into place in Chang's brain. "Maybe you can," he almost shouted. "I just remembered! All these big birds carry operational manuals with them. Let me look."

In a moment he found them, a sizeable row of black-bound volumes leaning together. It was like the California gold discovery; suddenly there was a way out, something to tell them, step by step, what to do and how it could be done. He leafed through them quickly, looking for engine start. Sylvester interrupted him.

"Look at the co-pilot's seat—the checklist! It's on rollers in that little box there. We can go down the checklist and be sure that everything is right; we won't have to guess at anything."

Chang looked up. "That's great. Listen—with these manuals, with the checklist, I think we can do it. I mean, I feel a lot better about it, a lot more confident—how about you?"

"Right. Suppose you find the engine-starting procedure. When you've got it, come up here, take the co-pilot's position, and we'll do the whole checklist. It'll take some time, but it's the only thing that makes any sense. There'll also be a pretaxi list, a runup check, and a preflight list. If we do them all, we ought to be in pretty good shape."

Chang's hands were trembling. "Let's get at the checklist. I'll bring the manual with me. We'll learn something from that; if we get through it all right, then we can fire up."

Sylvester nodded his approval. Chang undid his seat belt, which he had been careful to fasten, took the co-pilot's position, and adjusted the chair to his satisfaction.

"Number one item, before you even start reading, is to get the cabin door properly closed and the steps rolled away. Ask the Father to do that, will you? It will be a polite way of getting him off the aircraft."

"I can feel him walking around," Chang said.

"Yes, so can I."

"I'll get him off," Chang assured. "Four of us on board is enough necks to risk with what we are going to try and do. Agreed?"

"Completely." Sylvester continued to study the complicated panel, placing the position of every instrument he could recognize.

Chang climbed out of his chair, walked through the crew compartment, and opened the door to the cargo hold.

Twelve men he had never seen before were sitting on the floor with their backs to the sides of the fuselage. They had no seat belts and were lined up like tenpins.

"What's this?" Chang demanded.

Two of the men shook their heads to indicate they did not understand the language and pointed behind them. In mounting anxiety Chang opened the door to the passenger compartment.

Most of the seats were already filled: by women holding things on their laps, by children with their seat belts carefully fastened, by a few men who sat with what were obviously their families. At the rear door tall Father Ferrara was directing a woman with a baby in her arms to a vacant seat halfway up the aisle.

There were close to seventy people already on the airplane and more were waiting on the outside steps to come in.

Chang forced his way down the aisle, past the closely packed-in passengers, all of whom looked up at him when he went by, and a few of whom smiled. When he reached the doorway a sense of panic was tearing at his chest.

"Father, what have you done!" he demanded.

The priest looked down on him, a pillar of innocence with a sense of authority. "It is all right," he assured with unblinking calm. These people are the workers at the airport and their families. They know that the hurricane is a mighty one and that it is coming straight to us. They knew that the big plane was about to leave and they came to be saved also. In their small houses they could not survive the hurricane. There is no other place to go and there will be no food for the babies and the children. I have advised them it is best to come and they are now all here."

Chang was too overcome to think coherently. "Did you count them?" he asked in a hollow voice.

The priest smiled. "There are seventy-eight. As soon as we are all seated, we shall pray for the success of this trip. Have no fear; God will guide you, we shall all bless you, and you will take us to safety."

"Father, we can't . . ." Chang began.

The priest raised his hand. "I know what you are about to say. I cannot ask them to get off to lose their lives in the great storm which is now already beginning to be felt. There is no one else to come and save us; no other flying company stops here. Now we must together trust in God. The plane can carry us easily; otherwise there would not be the seats. And there is no cargo."

Chang tried once more. "The responsibility . . ."

The priest cut him off sharply with a gesture. "It is not in your hands, or mine. It rests with a higher Power. Accept it as it is. I will care for the people back here; be not afraid. All that you and Captain Sylvester have to do now is to fly the plane."

Chapter Six

ED CHANG FELT LIKE A MAN CAUGHT IN THE
path of an avalanche, faced with mounting forces totally beyond his power to arrest, and compelled to do something to
escape their fury. In the tall priest he recognized an almost
immovable obstacle. He felt that it would be a futile waste of
time and words to try to explain to him once more that two
reasonably well-qualified light plane pilots could be and
were hopelessly out of their depth in attempting to fly a
Constellation. The priest was asking Divine aid and was sure
that it would resolve the problem.

Chang accepted the thing which had been thrust upon
him with as much calmness of spirit as he could muster.
There were some immediate steps to be taken and he got on

with the job. He gave orders calmly with as much assurance in his manner as though he were, in fact, a fully-qualified first officer of a modern multi-engine airliner.

"Father, I need two men to help me. You said these people work here at the airport. Get me a couple who know what they are doing."

Two men arose from their seats close to the rear without being summoned. "What is it you want, Lieutenant?" one of them asked in good English.

"Go inside the terminal," Chang instructed. "In the cargo room there is a small aircraft. On the rear seat you will find a computer and underneath it a chart of the Caribbean. I want them both. Also this rolling stairway is a valuable piece of equipment. Put it on its side if you can and secure it firmly to the concrete posts in front of the building. After you do that, use the emergency ladder to return to the aircraft." He pointed to the place where it was fastened above the doorway.

"I will also pull out the landing gear pins after the engines are started," the man added. "I do this many times."

That gave Ed Chang a bad start. He knew, but he had forgotten, that the landing gears on airliners had locking pins inserted on the ground to prevent a possible accidental folding and consequent serious damage to the airframe and propellers. If the pins were not pulled, then the gear could not be retracted in flight, which would be almost as bad. What else, he wondered, would they overlook, or fail to do because of lack of knowledge? His new-found confidence was suddenly badly shaken.

It helped a little when the two men hurried to do his bidding. They trusted him, at any rate, and his authority was unquestioned. He returned to the cockpit, fighting with the problem of informing Dick Sylvester about the unexpected passenger load. Dick had all on his mind that he could be expected to handle; one more curve and his nerve might snap under the pressure of the responsibility and the inevitable knowledge of his own inadequacy for the job he was about to attempt.

"When in doubt," Chang said to himself inaudibly, "shut up." It was a rule which had served him well in the past. He decided to mention the passengers calmly, but not until the time seemed right to do so. He opened the door to the crew compartment and closed it carefully behind him.

Dick Sylvester still sat with his eyes on the panel before him, taking in every detail of the arrangement of the instruments, the controls, and the radio equipment—the working tools on which he would have to depend. Chang slid silently into the co-pilot's seat and fastened the lap belt.

"Let's do the checklist," Sylvester said in a curiously flat voice. Chang caught his mood and responded to it immediately.

The lieutenant reached up and turned the little roller box until the heading that he wanted showed. "Before-starting-engines checklist," he announced. "First item is ignition; it should be off."

Captain Sylvester looked over his head and touched the four switches with his left hand. "Good," he answered. "No problem there. I spotted them; they're just like Betsy's."

Chang did not comment. "*Seat belt* and *no smoking* signs. They're to be on."

"We can skip that, I think. By the way, did you get Father Ferrara off all right?"

Chang felt a sudden sweat. He carefully steadied himself before replying, and made his voice casual. "No, he insisted on looking after the passengers. He knows the risk, but I couldn't throw him off bodily. I decided we had enough to worry about."

Sylvester looked across at him. "Strange he would leave his flock at a time like this, but that's his problem. I'm not going to worry about it. I can't. What's the next item?"

Chang allowed himself to breathe again. "Auxiliary boost, to be checked and off."

"What auxiliary boost?" Sylvester asked.

"I don't know."

"Well, since it's supposed to be off, it can't be something we've got to have."

Chang foresaw problems and decided to avoid them if possible. He turned the scroll knob and read the full list to himself. "I don't see anything vital here we have to do," he concluded. "The landing gear is supposed to be down and it certainly is. Things like that."

"I don't think we should cut any corners," Sylvester said distinctly. "The checklist is there for a purpose. Things we plain don't understand about we can't do; those we can do, we should."

Chang took the rebuke and carefully read off, one by one, the fourteen remaining items. Nine of them they succeeded in verifying. The brake selector was on emergency, the deicer switches, which were labeled, were vacuum and off, the gyro compass was set. The elevator boost they could not locate, the hand pump they could not identify, and they had no way of verifying the CG.

Sylvester spoke carefully. "Every item we could find was in the proper position. I'm going to assume that the rest are too. If you don't agree with this, then we'll take the manual, dig out the information, and verify every one."

Ed Chang looked out at the pounding surf which testified to the rising wind and shook his head. "I'll buy it as is. That wind is definitely gaining and before we get going time may be critical."

"All right, then let's see if we can start the engines. I can't find any starters here, so they must be at the flight engineer's station."

Chang released the seat belt and sat down before the hopelessly complex maze of instruments and controls. He opened the manual and turned the pages for instructions. When he found them, he kept his voice as flat as Sylvester's had been. "I have a long checklist, thirty items. This is going to take me a while. However, I've got a picture of all the panels with everything marked, so it won't be too bad. I'll let you know if I miss anything or can't find it."

"Can I help?" Sylvester asked.

"Better not," Chang advised. "I've got to learn where things are and this is a good way to do it. Incidentally, I've found the engine starter controls, so that should be easy."

Sylvester allowed himself to relax for a moment and look out the window. Then he tensed in his seat. "Hey, there are two fellows out there tying down the cabin steps. Did you know about that?"

"Yes," Chang answered. "Two of the airport workers showed up. I sent them for my chart and computer, and told them to secure the steps. Also one of them is going to pull the landing gear pins after the engines are started."

Sylvester paled. "I never thought of that," he admitted.

Chang used his head. "Don't worry, it's on the checklist and we would have been sure to catch it." He kept on with his work, reaching up from time to time to check that a lever or switch was positioned as required. He spent ten full minutes in verifying, a job which Sylvester was intelligent enough not to interrupt.

The lieutenant finished and turned his head. "All done," he announced, "and again, everything was where it was supposed to be. As far as I'm concerned, we're ready to start engines."

For some reason Chang's assurance gave a lift to Sylvester's sagging morale. The ten long minutes had given him time to think, and the thoughts which had come were ominous and foreboding.

He turned and took hold of the controls for a moment. "Let's go," he said. "I've got the ignition switches, but you said you have the starters."

"That's right. Now the manual says that each engine must turn six blades before the ignition is turned on. The firing order is three, four, two, and one, the starting order, I mean. So when I call for it, give me ignition on number three engine. Got it?"

"I have," Sylvester answered. He looked up again at the four ignition switches.

"Stand by," Chang said. He reached over and turned on the master battery switch. There was a reaction from the panel before him, and on the one which faced the pilots' seats. Small lights came on and the aircraft seemed to come alive. Chang set the engine starting selector to 3, and pressed the starting button. Then he turned his head quickly and looked out the small window in the crew door. "Turning!" he announced triumphantly. "One, two, three, four, five, six . . ."

Sylvester flipped the ignition switch.

"Eight, niner, ten, eleven, twel . . ." A bark from the

engine cut him off. A dense cloud of smoke surrounded the nacelle and then blew away. Out the window Chang could see the silver arc of the propeller as it cut a disc pattern through the air.

This sign of life, this proof that they could command the latent power of the great airliner, surged like a magic elixir through the two CAP officers. They were both gripped by an eagerness now to prove their worth; they had chosen this dangerous and uncharted path, and the first big step was a success.

Chang held up four fingers and Sylvester nodded. The lieutenant turned the selector to 4, hit the starter button, and counted aloud. At six Sylvester turned on the ignition; at sixteen, after a heart-stopping few seconds, number four caught and settled down to a smooth idle.

In front of Chang, on the panel, gauges came to life and showed that numbers three and four were in operation. With soaring confidence Chang held up two fingers and repeated the successful process. When three engines were running he eased back on the throttles on his console to an indicated 1,000 rpm. Then, as though he had been doing it all of his life, he started number four. Presently a man stepped in front of the nose of the aircraft and held up three locking pins, with small red flags attached, for Sylvester to see. That done, he pulled the chocks and displayed them also. In a way it too was reassuring; the departure was taking place in a normal and professional manner.

In a few seconds a red light on the panel which indicated *Door Open* went out. Sylvester did not see it; he was occupied fitting a headset and setting the microphone adjustment to put the instrument next to his lips. He tried the pushbutton and it worked. Chang, seeing him, picked one of three available sets, tried it on, and found that the intercom was indeed working.

"Before-taxi checklist," he announced. "What emergency brake pressure do you show?"

After a moment Sylvester answered, "Seventeen hundred, I think."

"Good. Chocks and landing gear pins."

"Removed, I saw them."

"Clocks and altimeters."

"Set."

"NESA power switch, whatever that is."

While Sylvester searched, Chang reviewed the few items on his own list. He did not turn on the engine analyzer because he knew he could not read the wave patterns on the scope. He turned on the inverters after checking the manual text and reported. "Flight engineer, ready to taxi."

Remembering that the steps were safely out of the way, Sylvester pressed his feet forward on the rudder pedals and released the parking brake. At once the great long silver bird began to inch forward; he stopped it with a slight pressure on the upper part of the pedals.

His spirits lifted once more. The Connie worked exactly as Betsy did—push together to release, toes down for braking action. Cautiously he turned the nosewheel steering and released the brake pressure. Obediently the 116 feet plus of the fuselage, the 123 feet of the wide wingspan, and the four mighty turbo-compound, eighteen-cylinder engines responded to his command. The huge airliner began to turn with infinite grace toward the taxiway and the south end of the runway. Pulling his own throttle controls full back to keep his speed on the ground to a cautious minimum, Captain Sylvester for the first time in his life began to taxi a multi-engine aircraft.

A voice sounded in his ears. "Shall I stay here or come up for the take-off?"

"Stay there for runup and the checklist, then come up," he answered. He knew it was a sound decision. He could taxi without help and much of the runup would have to be the flight engineer's responsibility.

He surprised himself at how easily he taxied the aircraft, immense in comparison to anything he had ever flown. Yet it rolled easily down the taxiway, responded quickly to the nosewheel steering and was apparently indifferent to the decided crosswind. Sylvester overcontrolled a little as he tried to keep the plane straight on the taxiway, and knew it, but by the time he had reached the turning at the end he had already improved.

He leaned forward, looked up as best he could, and checked for any traffic in the pattern. He saw nothing. With calm assurance he touched the left brake and turned the nosewheel with his left hand. The big bird swung through ninety degrees and a bit more. Embarrassed, he corrected and carefully crossed the end of the runway to the runup area on the other side. He wanted to nose into the crosswind, as he would in a light aircraft.

He had some unexpected trouble turning the big plane on the runup cement, but at last he managed after very nearly running one main landing gear off onto the soil. He reflected grimly that he could not back up; next time he would do it better. He pushed forward with his toes and set the parking brake.

"Runup," he announced.

"I've got six pages of checklist," Ed answered. "I'll be a

while. The engines have to warm anyway. I'll tell you right now that without this manual we'd have been dead." He went to work with no further comment.

While he was waiting Dick Sylvester began to flex the controls, testing them for freedom of movement as he always did in any aircraft he was about to fly. The ailerons, invisible to him, responded smoothly; so did the rudder. The elevator was another matter; it was hard to move and showed no desire to cooperate. Unlike the other controls, however, it did not have balanced surfaces, but rather the uncompensated up-and-down motion of a substantial piece of aircraft structure. That would account for it, and Sylvester felt easier in his mind. He experienced now a considerable calmness, a quiet confidence that he was not, after all, in over his head. He thought that perhaps Father Ferarra's blessing was indeed being felt—he was no person to deny the power of Divine aid. He shut his eyes for a moment and let his lips move.

"Checklist completed," Chang reported. "Everything seems to be fine. I'm not trying to use the engine analyzer: I don't know how."

"That's all right," Sylvester agreed.

"A.O.K. Are your flight controls free?"

"Checked and free."

"De-icer boots off."

"I can't find them." He looked out at the leading edge of the wing. "No visible action. I'm sure they're off."

"Turn on the pilot heater switch."

Sylvester found it and did so.

"All set for runup," Chang reported. "Engines show warm according to the manual."

Sylvester checked the parking brake once more. "I'll run

up from here," he advised. "I don't have too much room and I want to be able to chop power fast if she starts to walk away with me. So hang on."

"You've got it," Chang responded. He leaned back and made a point of folding his arms.

The cargo cabin door opened and Father Ferrara appeared. Sylvester saw him and pulled one of the earphones out of the way to listen.

"I have the passengers all tied down," he reported. "The door is tight shut and locked; one of the men checked it. Everyone is happy and praying for your success. God bless you."

He returned to the cabin and closed the door behind him.

"What did he say? About men?" Sylvester asked, confused.

"The man who pulled the pins checked the door. He works here. He knows how."

Sylvester was still confused but did not press it. This was not a time for debating. Instead he fed the throttle forward on number one engine with great caution and listened for an answering roar of power. When it came he checked the right and left magnetos and then eased the power back. Number two he treated in the same way, but it seemed to cough slightly when it was asked for power.

With increased confidence he ran up numbers three and four with successful results; all eight magnetos appeared satisfactory.

"Take two and three again," Chang advised. "You only had them up to sixteen hundred and number two sounded a little rough to me." He kept the anxiety out of his voice, but the mystery of the ready airliner left on the ramp was back once more revolving inside his mind. If anything was wrong, now was the time to find it out—on the ground.

"I'll take them together," Sylvester said. "I've noticed they usually do it that way. If there is any difference, it should show up." Carefully he pushed the two inner throttles forward.

The engines roared into power. As the propellers bit into the air the whole airframe shook for an instant and then in what seemed a mighty spring it lurched forward and up—and froze there as though it were hanging on the brink of eternity.

Sylvester went white and jammed his feet against the brakes. Chang grabbed the edges of the desk before him and his mouth opened—he held back the impulse to scream because he did not dare to do so. The engines continued to slash the air; the plane remained motionless.

"What happened?" Chang asked when he could find and control his voice.

Sylvester had not yet recovered himself. Carefully he pulled the throttles back; when they had come halfway the whole great airliner appeared to jump backward three or four feet.

"I don't know," he admitted finally. "I thought the gear had collapsed or the brakes had failed, but she seems O.K. now."

"How do you feel?" Chang asked. He himself had had the scare of his life.

"I'm frightened."

Chang understood. He released his seat belt and climbed up into the co-pilot's station. He set the chair into position and looked out down the runway.

"Let's get the hell out of here, before anything else happens," he said, and somehow found the means to muster up a grin.

Sylvester was still badly shaken.

"We probably skidded on an oil patch," Chang added. He knew it was untrue, but it might get by.

Perhaps it did. With a major effort Sylvester forced himself to settle down and to try the controls experimentally once more.

"We've got to get that little girl to a doctor," he heard Chang say, "before the morphine wears off. There isn't any more."

Silently Sylvester nodded as though accepting the judgment of a court he could not hope to influence or escape. "Do you want to make the take-off?" he asked. "I just bungled something awfully."

"You're on the left-hand side, and you've got more than twice the experience, *Captain* Sylvester." Chang put an acid bite into his words. "Now live up to that uniform you're wearing, and those wings on your chest. What the hell do you think the United States Air Force is, a bunch of sissies?"

Sylvester turned and looked hard over his left shoulder up at the traffic pattern; he avoided looking at the long heavy span of the wing. There was no traffic. He turned the nosewheel sharply to the left and released the brakes. Obediently the massive aircraft turned slowly toward the runway and began to move out onto the strip. Sylvester swung the steering wheel hard right and the Constellation pivoted until it was facing down the runway toward the water at the far end. A mile of smooth concrete stretched its invitation to the pilots and to their waiting aircraft.

Dick Sylvester had sat like this many times, never so far off the ground, and on every previous occasion a secret thrill had run the length of his spine to tell him that he was going to fly. That he *could* fly. That after years of hoping and waiting he had at last become a pilot, and had received his inheritance in the highways of the sky.

The familiar emotion returned now. Dick Sylvester found himself as he looked at the black pattern of tire burns before him made by countless landing aircraft. There was only one thing he could do now.

"Let's go," he said.

"Let's go," Chang repeated. It was harder for him, because he too was a pilot and he could not have the comfort of feeling his hands on the controls.

Captain Sylvester held the brakes hard while he pushed the throttles all the way forward. The heavy engines responded with a Niagara of sound and suppressed power; the air screamed under the agony of the racing propellers.

"God help us," Sylvester said, and released the brakes.

The Constellation surged forward, pressing the pilots back into their seats. With one hand on the control yoke and the other on the nosewheel steering Dick Sylvester did his best to keep the accelerating tons of weight on a straight heading down the rapidly shortening runway. The speed mounted, and the aircraft began to swing to the side. As he would have in a light plane Sylvester pushed the opposite rudder and the huge plane responded. He felt it begin to grip the air as he held the ailerons hard into the crosswind. He felt the beginning of a rise in the landing gear; the weight was coming onto the wings. Ahead the runway was disappearing fast as the water rushed nearer; he could see the breakers now and their anger as they flung their spray higher, much higher than before, against the rocks. They waited with cold hatred for the rushing aircraft, ready to swallow it whole and to smash it on the heavy rocks.

Dick Sylvester was rolling faster than he ever had before

on the ground and the opposite end of the runway was rushing to meet him. He seized the wheel and pulled back to lift the nose into the sky.

The plane did not respond.

In desperation, and sudden, uncontrolled panic, he pulled like a madman, but the Super-Constellation continued its roaring plunge down the runway. Five hundred feet of pavement remained, then the water.

Ed Chang watched and measured; because he was not flying he was free to see everything which went on. He saw the desperate pullback and saw it fail. The elevators had not responded. In one single flash of consciousness he remembered his light plane training and diagnosed what might be wrong. He had no time to speak; in six seconds they would be in the water, the murderers of seventy-eight innocent people. Like a swordsman whose reflexes have been trained through years of intensive competition, he whipped up his left arm, seized the wheel which controlled the horizontal trim tab setting and yanked it back in a thirty-degree arc.

Before he could repeat the motion he felt the cockpit rise, saw the water rush up, and underneath, and heard that the roar of the four mighty engines had not stopped in sudden, violent disaster. The runway was behind them, they were still alive and whole, and he knew that they were in the air.

Chapter Seven /

"GEAR UP!" DICK SYLVESTER COMMANDED.

He allowed himself that bit of drama because he had thought about it beforehand; if he got the plane successfully into the air, it would be his reward.

Ed Chang reached down and grasped the gear handle on the center pedestal. It refused to come up. He pushed, then pulled, which released it. There was a heavy thumping underneath the aircraft, then after several seconds the indicator on the panel before him showed the wheels to be up and locked. That done he looked out the window. There was angry water, two to three hundred feet below them, impotent to reach them where they were now. He leaned back to force himself to relax for a moment.

In an instant a blinding, head-splitting roar blasted through the cockpit. It was as if the door to the lowermost hell had suddenly been flung open and all the shrieks of the dammed were ringing in his ears. In stark fright he looked at his partner, who clung feverishly, his knuckles white, to the controls. Ed forced himself to locate the source of the unearthly noise; he found it in the window on his side of the cockpit—it had not been properly secured and it had blown partly open.

He grabbed the handle and locked it firmly into position. The noise ceased and as it did so a sense of order returned to the flight deck.

"It could have been worse," Sylvester said. He appeared to be beyond shock, in a world of his own where the only thing which mattered was the operation of a great airliner which he only slightly understood.

Ed swallowed hard and compelled himself to regain his composure. "How about the flaps?" he asked.

"Are they down?" There was surprise in Sylvester's voice.

"Sure, I set the flaps according to the before take-off checklist. Sixty percent. I thought you knew."

"I didn't. Raise them, slowly. I'm having a lot of trouble with the elevator control; it flops back and forth and then stops dead. I'm using the trim tab to hold the nose above the horizon."

"Flaps coming up."

Chang let them rise, stopped them for a few seconds, and then retracted them completely against the under surface of the wing. Sylvester made an adjustment in the trim tab setting and stared at the instrument panel.

"Now listen," he said carefully. "I'm going to hold a rate of climb of eight hundred feet a minute. I'm sure this bird can do three times that, but I'm going to go easy on everything. We aren't on a flight plan, but it's going to have to be Victor Fox Roger anyway because neither of us can fly instruments, let alone in this."

"Agreed," Chang said. Visual flight rules was the only possibility with their limited experience.

"We're headed between west and north, so we have to pick an even altitude, plus five hundred. I'm going to use eight thousand, five. That means we won't have to worry about superchargers, cabin pressurization, or any of the other systems we don't understand. Anything we don't absolutely need we leave alone—agreed?"

"Completely," Chang said. "That's a funny altitude for a Connie, but so what. I'd rather fly where we know what we are doing."

"Me too. How about the power setting; hadn't we better back off on these throttles a little?"

Immediately Chang realized that as flight engineer he had already committed a massive blunder. In light aircraft climbs at full power are normal; in engines where the horsepower is given in thousands full-throttle operation is only safe for a matter of seconds. He reached out to the duplicate set of throttles on the center pedestal and pulled them back about twenty-five percent.

"That's a guess," he said. "If it isn't enough power, let me know." He was the flight engineer, and it was his responsibility.

"If I need more, I'll take it," Sylvester said. "Ed, I think you better get back to the flight engineer's station and do the after take-off checklist if there is one. There may be other things besides the engines we have to reset. Then see if you can get a radio going. Try to get Miami Oceanic Control on one twenty-six decimal seven or one twenty-six decimal niner."

"Right." Chang released his seat belt and walked back the two or three steps to the engineer's console. His sense of responsibility grew as he sat down and realized that most of the operation of the complicated airliner rested in his hands, that his reading of the manual was vital to their success.

He found the brief checklist and went through it carefully. There was nothing difficult except cowl flaps, which he did not know how to set. He consulted the manual and after flipping many pages back and forth found what he needed. Almost as though he were reaching for the forbidden fruit, and enjoying it, he set in thirty degrees of cowl flap on each engine. It was his baby and he would rock it.

"Hey, Ed, how about a heading?" came over his headset. "I'm holding three six zero at the moment, but I know that isn't right."

"Right away," Chang answered, and got up. He slipped through the crew door into the cargo hold. It was as bleak and bare as before, an aluminum cave with heavy pressed ribs and stringers to hold it in shape. A full dozen silent men sat on the floor, some of them with their backs against the rear bulkhead. One was on his feet looking unbelievingly out the window at the clouds and the water below.

Chang walked briskly down the length of the long compartment, trying his best to convey a sense of confidence and security, flashed a quick smile at the men who were watching him, and opened the door to the passenger compartment.

It was crammed with humanity. Father Ferrara, looking taller than ever, was standing midway up the aisle beside a woman who held a crying baby in her arms. Ed had to stop for a moment beside the litter over the first row of seats on which Armando lay, his face now tight with pain. The lieutenant laid a hand on his shoulder and received an effort at a smile in return.

"You saving my life," Armando said, and then gave up the attempt at conversation. He twisted his body a little and resigned himself to the long, agonizing parade of minutes end to end which would last until the aircraft was on the ground somewhere in the United States. Across from him the little girl with the burned body slept fitfully under the influence of the narcotic she had been given. Chang looked at her for several seconds, studying the dark, innocent outlines of her small immature features and wondered what the future held for her, how much pain she would have to endure, and whether she would live. He gave silent thanks for the Navy medico who had supplied the morphine which was sparing her so much now, and turned his attention to Father Ferrara, who was waiting to speak to him.

"A beautiful take-off," the priest said with a smile of confidence and trust. "We were frightened for a moment when the brakes slipped and threw us about somewhat, but all is fine now. It is wonderful to fly, like the angels. It is my first time in an airplane."

Chang had not thought of that possibility ."Are there any other first flighters?" he asked, not that it made any great difference.

"Almost everyone is flying for the first time. And it is a beautiful ride. Many saints have been asked to bless us, and especially the three for whom the airport is so finely named."

The lieutenant did not risk speech after that. He retrieved his computer and chart from the man who had brought them on board in answer to his instructions, and returned to the flight bridge. There he seated himself at the engineer's desk, unfolded his well-worn chart, and studied it carefully.

He put on the headset and spoke. "Fly three two zero degrees."

"Wilco," Sylvester answered. There was a new tone in his voice, a touch of authority and confidence. He moved the horizontal stabilizer slightly with his right hand. "We are passing five thousand and climbing. The power setting is good as far as I can tell. I've tried to synchronize the engines. Everything looks fine."

Chang responded in kind, everything did seem to be right and, whatever the odds, they were airborne and Dick was doing splendidly at the flight controls. He was ready to cover all bets they would make a smooth, greased-on landing and would taxi in like two of the best pros in the business. What the hell, a pilot was a pilot—either you could fly or you couldn't. They could. He pressed his lips together in grim satisfaction.

The headset came alive. "Ed, I need some help. This damn elevator is worse than useless. It isn't tight at all; it flops a few degrees and then stops cold. Something's kaput. Read up and see what you can do. I'm holding her with the trim tab, but I sure as hell can't land her this way!"

The optimistic mood burst like a bubble. With one full third of the control system not operating, something was radically wrong.

By consulting the manual he found the elevator boost control. It was in the off position. "I've got it!" he declared, and flipped the overhead switch to ON.

"No change," Dick said after a half minute had passed.

Chang tried the emergency boost control on the left side

of the center pedestal. Again there was no success. He turned them back off. "I don't know what it is," he confessed. "I've read that section of the manual through twice. Does it work at all?"

"Not so you'd notice it."

"I'll see what else I can find," he offered.

"I've got a better idea," Sylvester said. "You come up here and fly this thing for a while. We'd both better get used to it before we come in for a landing. I'll take a look at the manuals and see if I can find something you might have missed."

That was fine with Ed Chang. He climbed into the co-pilot's position with a renewed sense of importance. When he had everything adjusted to his satisfaction he nodded that he was ready to take over; Dick Sylvester held up his hands to indicate that he was relinquishing the controls. As Ed settled down to guiding the multi-engine aircraft through the sky, he hoped that his partner wouldn't suddenly take it into his mind to go to the back latrine. If he did, he would find one hell of a surprise when he hit the passenger cabin.

Miss Doris Beverly Wong settled down with natural grace and picked up the telephone. She fitted the listening end of the instrument against her shapely ear, brushed her sleek black hair out of the way, and dialed with one tapered, slender finger. As she waited for the answer a pleasant, impish smile touched the corners of her mouth and gave a fresh character to her pert and beautifully molded features. As she sat, twisted slightly in her chair, she looked like a particularly delectable example of oriental femininity, which was precisely what she was.

The answering voice came over the line with brisk formality: "Civil Air Patrol, Sergeant Grossman."

"This is Miss Wong," Doris said, in a warm voice. "May I speak to Lieutenant Chang, please."

There was a bare moment's hesitation on the line. "Who did you say was speaking, please?"

"Miss Wong, Miss Doris Wong."

"One moment, Miss Wong."

This time the pause was considerably longer—they were getting him. A full minute passed and then a voice came on the line which was not the one she was expecting to hear. It was heavier and more mature. "This is Colonel Williams. May I help you?"

Doris cooled her voice a little. "I'm sorry, Colonel, I was calling for Lieutenant Chang. They must have given me the wrong extension."

"No, I'd like to speak to you for a moment if I may. Is this a member of Lieutenant Chang's family?"

The fingers of Doris' left hand tightened around the instrument and her knuckles went white. It was not the words she had heard but the way in which they had been spoken that had alarmed her. "Lieutenant Chang's family as far as I know is all in Hawaii." She fought to keep her voice level. "I am . . . a close friend." She could restrain herself no longer. "Is anything wrong?"

"I didn't catch your name."

"Doris Wong."

"Lieutenant Chang is not here at the moment, Miss Wong. I don't wish to alarm you in any way, but he is overdue on a flight which went out early this morning. We are quite certain that he and Captain Sylvester have landed at an alternate airport; we're checking them now. Meanwhile we have several other search planes out in the area he was covering, so I'm sure he will be all right."

The smile had abruptly vanished from Doris' face; tenseness rapidly began to fill every part of her slender body and her whole world became the voice on the other end of the telephone.

"Where did he go, Colonel?" she demanded.

"Lieutenant Chang and Captain Sylvester went out on a routine search and rescue mission about eight hours ago. We had a report that four Cuban fishermen were floating in an open rubber life raft; Lieutenant Chang took off to try and locate them."

"Could he still be out there?" Doris asked, knowing the answer she would receive.

"Not with his original gas load, Miss Wong, no. He and Captain Sylvester landed somewhere, we know that. We are waiting for a message from them now. Or, of course, they may have simply gassed up, gone back to the search area, and will be coming in at any time."

The words did not carry the conviction they sought to convey, even though they were spoken in a conversational tone.

"Colonel." Doris tried to control her voice. "Ed is my boy friend. It's more than that. We've been going together for some time and . . ." She could not finish.

"I understand, Miss Wong. If you will give me your number, I'll call you the moment they arrive back or we hear from them."

It wouldn't do, not for a moment. "I can't wait. May I come out there, please?"

"If you want to. Give your name to the guard at the gate and he will direct you. Ask for me, Colonel Williams."

"Yes, sir." Doris hurried the words, hung up, and crushed her small hands into tight fists. Then she forced herself to be calm, to remember where she had left her purse, and the keys to her little car. But the cork popped out of what composure she had left, she fled to grab her things, and in less than a minute her shaking fingers were trying to fit the ignition key into the lock. She had not even glanced into the mirror to see her usually rewarding reflection; her mind had narrowed to the route to the airport, to the fastest possible way to get there, and to the thought that perhaps by the time she arrived that overly lean frame and slightly hollow-cheeked face she had come to know so well would be there and her heart could start beating once again.

Scotty Zimmerman was dead tired when he at long last lined up his final approach for the hot runway at Miami International and lowered the gear for the landing. He had worked throughout most of the previous night loading gear and equipment onto the DC-3, and the flight up from Tres Santos had been rugged. The weather had let up a little as far as the Yankee Route was concerned, but the hurricane alert had doubled and tripled the normally substantial traffic load coming into the southern Florida peninsula.

His clearance in via Nassau had been long and involved—he had had to hold Lizzie in the pattern waiting his turn while every aching muscle in his body had demanded relief and rest. The one bright spot had been Lizzie herself: as practically always she had flown with endless patience and without any demands for herself at all. The trip was almost over now and in another five minutes or so he could climb out of the seat where he earned his living and think about something else.

Galloway seemed to take little if any interest in the landing. He showed no disposition to make it himself. If he had, Scotty would have relinquished the controls in a moment. But Galloway still sat in the co-pilot's chair, looking ahead with eyes which seemed to ignore what they saw, and with his fingertips drumming on the windowsill. That was a bad sign, when Galloway started drumming like that. It meant that something was worrying him very much.

Scotty brought the faithful DC-3 down the glide path, flared, and put her on for the five or six hundredth time. Lizzie slowed down, let her tail drop onto the runway and turned off at the first taxiway. The choice parking spots closest to the main terminal building were reserved for Pan American, Eastern, and the other big carriers. Scotty taxied on past and down toward the end where a collection of other piston-engined aircraft marked the operating area of the lesser airlines. He swung her around, put her onto the blocks, and cut the engines. As the veteran aircraft came to a stop he snapped the few switches which had to be shut down and let silence take possession of the cockpit. It was close to complete except for the soft staccato of Bob Galloway's fingertips, which still beat out a pattern on the windowsill.

"Let's go," Scotty said. "I'm tired and I want something to eat."

Galloway came to. "I'm sorry," he answered. "You and the boys go on in. I'll join you after I make a phone call."

When they got off the aircraft Scotty signaled the others to leave Galloway alone. When Wilson indicated that he would go with him, Herb Stallings held out his muscular arm and blocked his way. Something very decidedly was on Galloway's mind and Herb knew exactly what it was.

With his thoughts clearly miles away Bob walked into the terminal and closeted himself in a phone booth. He checked a number in a small leather pocket notebook he carried, put in his money, and spun the dial. When he got an answer he said, "Mr. Wettstein, please," and waited. His fingers drummed a pattern on the little gray shelf in the booth.

When Wettstein came on the line Galloway's speech was crisp and clear. "Bob Galloway. Sam, I don't like to disturb you at home on a Sunday, but I have to check something with you right away."

"Of course, Bob," Wettstein answered. "Any time. Go ahead."

"I want to know what my insurance position is." He described what was wrong with the Connie and the way they had left her. "I've been having second thoughts all the way up here, and I'm just about going out of my mind. Right now I'm seriously considering going back down there and getting her. I was a fool to let Herb Stallings talk me into doing what I did."

"I'm not so sure about that," Wettstein said. "Now let me get this straight. The elevator boost is entirely out, and there is no back-up system, is that right?"

"Yes."

"I don't know too much about Connies; I never flew them myself. How would the controls react under these circumstances? Could you use the elevator by muscle power to a satisfactory degree?"

"No, because in a boost-out condition the yoke would

flop back and forth several degrees instead of holding tight, and then if you got any reaction it would take a great deal of power to produce it."

"Well, in that case, Bob, how did you propose to get her out of there?"

"On the trim tab. It can be done that way. It's a lot more work, of course, but any experienced Connie pilot could do it. Herb brought her in in just that condition."

"And what has you worried is that the company may take the attitude that you should have brought her out, regardless of her condition, in the face of the severe hurricane warning."

"That pretty much sums it up. Plus the fact that I can't stand the idea of a damned good airplane getting smashed up because of my carelessness or too hasty decision."

"Relax, and let me point something out to you. If Herb Stallings red-lined the aircraft as unsafe to fly, then it would be a violation for anyone to attempt to move her in that condition. Now add to that the heavy congestion I know we've got in this area right now, with everything with wings that isn't Communist coming up from the Caribbean, and the weather conditions in the face of a hurricane, and you'll see that trying to bring that ship in here would do nothing but get you into a peck of trouble."

"That's what Herb said," Galloway admitted.

"All right. Now you know, if you've read your policy, that if you do anything which is a deliberate violation of the FAA regulations, your coverage is automatically voided. Anything serious, that is. Flying a red-lined aircraft certainly comes under that heading. I can't officially speak for the company on this, but if you can prove that the Connie is red-lined, and for a legitimate reason, then leaving her as you did was the only thing you *could* do and you're covered for the replacement cost of the aircraft or whatever repair charges are required to put her back in shape, minus the repairs on the control boost system. You could certainly give them a hell of an argument if they saw it any other way."

"The Connie is red-lined all right, but the only witnesses I have to that fact are my own employees."

"Then in that case the company may ask that its own specialist examine the aircraft, or the wreckage if it is destroyed, and confirm the hydraulic failure. Of course you face no problem there."

"Thanks," Galloway said.

"Now as a personal friend," Wettstein went on, "take my advice and don't go back down there and try to do anything heroic. The blow is a big one and it's moving rapidly according to the last report I heard. If it comes down to that, I'll take the witness stand and testify that when you consulted me I gave you this advice."

"That isn't worrying me," Galloway retorted. "I just want to be absolutely sure that I won't be held negligent for not having the parts on hand to fix the boost system or for not bringing her out as she was."

"I've answered that. You would have voided your policy the moment you poured the coal at the end of the runway to take off, and when you landed the FAA boys would have been out in force for your scalp. You don't know when you're lucky. You're insured with a good company, so relax and forget it. Go eat a rare steak."

"Thanks," Galloway answered. "I'll do just that. I feel better now."

He walked out of the phone booth wondering if he would ever see Connie again. He realized that he probably loved her more than the wife who had left him more than twenty years ago. Connie took things as they came, and that was something Sheila had never been able to do.

Lieutenant Edmund Chang was in his element. After some twenty minutes he was convinced he had the feel of the Connie and that she was willingly obeying his instructions. He had schooled his left hand in the operation of the elevator trim tab control, and with that device he kept the big bird reasonably on altitude. The rudder and aileron controls were a cinch and the elevator, as soon as Dick Sylvester found how to turn on the right switch, would make everything Betsy all over again, in spades. A thought flashed through his mind and he wished mightily that a certain very attractive young lady could be there to see him and what he was doing.

He slipped a hand inside the pocket of his uniform, brought out a little sealed-in-plastic picture of Miss Doris Wong, and wedged it in place against the windshield.

"Never mind the doll; watch the gauges," Dick Sylvester advised.

"I can handle both," Chang answered with total confidence in his voice. Since the window episode he had recovered rapidly and his spirits now soared with the aircraft. He adjusted the elevator trim and checked the magnetic compass. He might well become the first Chinese-American multi-engine jet aircraft commander on the airways of the world. He was already a pilot and in calm, self-possessed control of a seventy-ton, twelve-thousand-horsepower airliner. Furthermore he had started the engines and it had been his own quick thinking which had saved the flight from what could have been a total take-off disaster.

He felt a touch on his shoulder. He turned his head, took one look, and felt the confident smile vanish from his face when he saw the grim look which Dick Sylvester had on his. Without a word Sylvester handed him the aircraft log book and pointed to the last items.

Chang read the carefully written words and agony seized him.

Complete elevator boost system failure while in flight. Aircraft emergency landed on trim tab control only. No passengers or cargo aboard. Aircraft unsafe and may not be flown under any circumstances until system repaired.

P. W. Sims, Flt/Eng.

H. R. Stallings, Capt. 45,554

And underneath, below the deadly red lines:

Visual inspection confirmed total hydraulic failure of elevator boost system. Aircraft grounded as unsafe to fly this date.

P. W. Sims, Flt/Eng.

Sylvester broke the silence. "We got ourselves into this and we have no one but ourselves to blame. But I'm thinking of Armando, and that little girl, and Father Ferrara. Back there we have three innocent human lives depending on us, and we're really in for it."

Chapter Eight /

THE FIRST OF THE TURBULENCE HIT THEM three minutes later. Up until that time the air had been relatively smooth despite the sustained force of the wind; now the pattern broke and the stability of the air mass abruptly changed.

The initial shock swept the great plane up as though it were on the crest of a huge wave. The airframe shook under the impact and Ed Chang, paling a little under his tan, suddenly had to battle the controls. For the first time he felt almost completely lost without the elevator, which is so vital in handling an aircraft in rough air. He fought with the trim tab, trying to make it compensate for the rough air and keep the plane on a constant altitude. This it refused to do and the Constellation wallowed in the buffeting, only partly under control.

When a sharp downdraft hit, Dick Sylvester was climbing into the left-hand pilot's seat; he had to hang on desperately to keep from being thrown backward into the cockpit. He managed to sit down and fasten his seat belt while Ed Chang, with a shaking left hand, corrected the attitude of the plane with the trim tab wheel.

In the cabin Father Ferrara raised his arms to motion that everyone should remain calm, then for the second time he left the crowded area and entered the cargo hold. The twelve men there were in a wild assortment of positions, each trying to hold on to something as best he was able. The priest attempted to walk up the center of the fuselage; he was halfway to the cockpit door when another major shock swept him off his balance and slammed him against the side of the cabin. He seized hold of one of the aluminum stringers and shut his eyes in pain. Then he recovered himself and very gingerly made his way toward the forward door. He opened it and stepped into the flight deck area.

"Is something wrong with the plane?" he asked, holding on to the tops of the two pilots' seats.

"This is rough air, Father," Chang answered. "We have to expect it with a hurricane in the area. It may get worse before it gets better." Despite the fact he knew that it was inoperative, he attempted to push the yoke forward, to bring down the nose of the airliner.

"It is very difficult for the passengers," Father Ferrara said with restraint. "Armando is crying in pain."

"If this keeps up too long," Sylvester offered, "I'll take her up to a higher altitude. But we would have less oxygen and it might not be any smoother up there."

"You will do what is necessary," the priest said, staring at the instrument panel. "But I cannot see how you can understand all of these controls and things. It is beyond my mind to comprehend them."

Sylvester made an effort to appear calm and confident. "You could learn, Father, but right now you are more valuable in the cabin. Tell Armando, and the little girl if she is awake, that the air is rough but that the plane is all right—almost," he added under his breath. "We will do all we can to keep it as smooth as we can, but some things we cannot control."

Which was true.

The priest raised his right hand and made the sign of the Cross in the air. He ignored the pain in his body where he had been smashed against the sidewall, and made his way back to the crammed cabin. When he had the door shut behind him he clapped his hands for attention and raised his voice enough to be heard.

"We are in angry air," he explained. "Because of this the plane is hard to control. Our pilots are doing their best and I have blessed them. We must be patient and endure. There is no danger."

As if in reply the heavy airframe shook again and the tall priest had to hang on desperately to keep his position in the aisle. A baby that had been asleep awoke abruptly and burst into a loud spasm of crying. Its mother patted it and tried to rock it back and forth, but it would not be comforted.

Father Ferrara bent low over the burned little girl, who was sleeping fitfully. He laid his extraordinarily long hand across her brow as though he could will her comfort and repose. Then he straightened up and reassured Armando with a brave smile. The young man paid no attention as the pains in his abdomen were cruel and for the moment they had taken complete control of his mind. The priest understood that the turbulence had aggravated Armando's condition and that every sudden jarring motion of the aircraft sharpened his agony.

He looked about the rest of the cabin to be sure that the remainder of his flock was in good order. He turned his eyes on a very old woman who sat wedged between her heavily-built son and his overly plump wife. Her eyes were dulled with the shock of this totally new experience and the unavoidable fright which the shuddering motions of the aircraft had so clearly induced. Father Ferrara spoke to her softly and earnestly in Spanish and patted her hand in reassurance. Across the aisle a young girl was being wretchedly sick into one of the heavy paper bags provided at each seat.

The plane hit another wrenching bump and the cabin heaved upward with a force that shook everyone in their seats. The air was thick and heavy from the close confinement of so many human bodies and the effects of the turbulence which had caused so many of them to perspire. In the very back a muscular laborer swayed as his substantial body was rocked by the motion of the aircraft. In his arms he held his most precious possession, a guitar which he had brought to be rescued along with himself. Because he had been a sailor the airsickness which was beginning to permeate the whole cabin had not yet begun to affect him; he clutched his instrument as though it might have been a child and tried to shield it from being struck by the back of the seat in front of him each time there was some new motion of the cabin.

Father Ferrara made his way, handhold by handhold, down the aisle and stood beside him. "Play," he commanded.

93

The laborer understood. He shifted the guitar into position and drew his thumb across the strings slowly two or three times as though he were waking it from a kind of sleep. Then, softly, he began a simple melody. After he had played it once through he started again and this time added his voice to the traditional Mexican tune, *La Borrachita*. Across the aisle from where he was sitting a much younger man who sat holding hands with his pregnant wife took it up in a clear tenor. More voices joined in the smooth flow of the romantic song. When the cabin heaved again from the force of the vertical drafts of the wind, the flow of the music was uninterrupted.

By the third time through almost everyone was singing, the thinner children's voices louder and braver than the rest. They sang with a cautious restraint which fitted the song of the little drunkard and the circumstances in which they all found themselves. The singing and the flow of the melody broke the grip of the fear which was beginning to charge the cabin and gave life to a new calmness which took its place. The crying baby at last subsided and fingers which had been gripping the arm rests in sharp fear gradually relaxed. The big plane shook once more, but no one seemed to care. The music had taken hold of them and given them something to think about and to do. The beauty of the gentle, flowing song filled the cabin with its peace. The baby pushed its tiny head against its mother and returned to sleep.

"We've got to get a radio going," Dick Sylvester said. "There must be ten of them on this thing; see what you can do and if you can raise Miami Oceanic Control. Do you know the frequency?"

"Of course," Chang answered shortly. He signaled the change-over to Dick, who took the controls, then he began to investigate the radio equipment within his reach.

It proved easier than he had expected. The VHF transceiver was at least a relative of the one in Betsy, an aircraft in which he was checked out to fly both solo and with a passenger. He turned to 126.7 and with more clarity than he had expected he picked up the traffic control center. The airwaves were crowded and communication was almost constant; he had never heard it so busy. He decided to attempt a transmission although he was sure he was still too far out to be heard, even with airline equipment and a sophisticated antenna system.

Sylvester nodded that he was receiving on his headset. "We're better off now," he said through the intercom. "In a little while we will be able to report in and close our old flight plan. They must be out looking for us right now, and if somebody goes in the water because we couldn't close out I'll never forgive myself no matter what happens."

"You did your best," Chang answered.

The radar air traffic controller who first saw the pip on his scope noted it. When the sweep of the antenna had marked it four or five times more, and there was no doubt that it was a target, he gave it closer attention. Around him a long row of hard-working, highly-skilled men were battling with the limited airspace and the heavy overload of incoming aircraft. It was a triumph of communications and technology that they kept everything straight and were successfully vectoring in a huge variety of aircraft, from slow private planes to multi-engine jets penetrating from high altitudes at 600-mph speeds.

The thing which made this particular pip interesting was the fact that it was not squawking—it was not putting out the prearranged signal which the transponder on board would send to the radar scope to identify it as friendly.

If an enemy attack were to come, the controller knew thoroughly, any kind of an unusual circumstance would make it more probable. A sudden surge of good will on the part of the Communist world. Christmas Eve. Or a hurricane alert off the coast of Florida.

He picked up his microphone, waited for a break, and went on the air: "Aircraft approaching Miami off-airways vector one four four degrees, speed two eight zero knots, if you read this transmission turn to a heading of three four zero degrees and squawk alpha zero two flash for radar identification. Maintain present altitude."

Captain Richard Sylvester heard him clearly. So did Lieutenant Chang. At the moment that the transmission came through the Super-Constellation caught the granddaddy of all the bumps it had hit so far; the cabin, the cockpit, the whole aircraft shot upward with stomach-wrenching force and the right wing rose alarmingly high in the air. Both pilots fought to return the plane to normal. Sweat made their hands wet on the control yoke and their hearts pounded at a rate far above normal. By the time they had the aircraft once more on an even keel and the instruments had settled down to normal readings, the message from Miami radar had come in again. But as far as they were concerned, someone somewhere was talking to the man in the moon.

When the second transmission was not acknowledged and no squawk appeared on the tube, the controller picked up one of four telephones at his elbow. He made three quick calls, the first two to other sections of air traffic control, the third to the Florida Air National Guard. The Guard, as always, was on the alert and standing by. When the report came in the scramble bell rang almost at once. Less than four minutes later two F-102 Delta Dagger supersonic jet interceptors lined up the runway in formation, revved up, hit their afterburners, and began to accelerate rapidly. At around 150 knots they lifted their nosewheels, held the attitude until they had flying speed, and came off. They quickly tucked up their wheels and in formation wheeled off in a war-readiness condition on a magnetic heading of one four nine degrees. As they climbed with great speed it was only a matter of a fairly short time until both of them had the unknown aircraft locked on their radar scopes. Underneath, in their pods, the armed rockets were ready and waiting.

At almost the same time the commander of an Air Rescue Service SA-16 Grumman amphibian flashed confirmation of a sighting. He arrived over a sea area where a Civil Air Patrol Stinson was orbiting and verified the location of a small rubber life raft on the tossing water below. Although the ARS pilot actually considered the possibility, a water landing was clearly out of the question. The Albatross rescue plane put out a call for a surface vessel and raised one only a scant seven miles away. The surface ship immediately altered course to make the pickup. The SA-16 released the CAP Stinson to return to base, but the pilot declined.

"Two of our own boys are down out here," he reported tersely. "We will continue our search pattern as long as possible."

"I have the same alert," the Grumman A/C responded. "As soon as we have this pickup made, we'll go after your boys." He pulled back on the power and descended to take as close a look as he dared at the rubber raft. One man lay in the bottom, one sat folded up caring nothing, two others waved feebly. The pilot felt the most rewarding emotion the rescue man can know, but at the same time he chalked this one up for the Civil Air Patrol. In his twin-engine amphibian he reflected that those guys had guts to go out over water in their little single-engine land planes. Now two of them were unreported and he wouldn't bet a dime on their chances. At the same time he would cheerfully have given everything he possessed to be allowed to find them and vector in a rescue vessel. As soon as he was free, he knew that he would put out his utmost effort for them as long as the light held.

For a little while Sylvester flew on in silence, while the ceaseless terse communications which flowed through his headset forced into his mind a realization of the navigational problems which lay before him. Miami, and the whole surrounding area, was jammed with traffic. The great bulk of it was operating under Instrument Flight Rules, with each aircraft having its flight path exactly set out and cleared before it according to strict regulations. Special training, and a special license, were required for IFR operations—neither of which he possessed. There was only one way out: he would have to establish communication with the Miami air traffic controllers and obtain permission to come in by picking his way visually and looking out for other aircraft as he did so. It was the only way he knew how to fly.

Across the narrow center console Ed Chang read his thoughts. Chang also was not qualified on instruments: the course was long and expensive and he simply had not had the money to take it. He gave some serious thought to the possibility of their going to some other place to land, but this created more problems than it solved. There was the question of where—the congested Miami area would have to be cleared in any case, darkness would be closing in before too long, and Armando could not wait very many more hours for medical attention. Chang decided once more to keep his mouth shut. They were doing all right so far, and if their luck held they would make it in somehow.

"Look!" Sylvester shouted, and pointed to the sky before them. Chang did look, and in a few seconds picked up the shapes of two jet fighters, which seemed to be aimed directly toward them. With his lean bony fingers Chang seized the control wheel. If it became necessary to swing the big Super-Constellation out of the way he might have to add his strength to help with the maneuver.

Just before a decision was imperative the jets peeled off and a few moments later whipped past the port side of the Connie.

"Wow!" Sylvester said. "I'm glad those guys were looking where they were going."

"Maybe not," Chang answered. "They may just have seen us on their radars and gone around that way. At least they're gone."

Less than half a minute later he knew he had been mistaken. Dick Sylvester did not speak; he simply pointed over his left shoulder. Ed looked and saw the two fighters, in close formation, sitting together off his wingtip. They had their gear extended to slow them down to the Connie's speed, and their trailing edge flaps were down. The sudden, sick realization hit Chang that the jets had come out specifically to intercept them—and that meant they were in immediate, deep, serious, and possibly dangerous trouble.

"What do we do?" he asked.

"We keep on flying straight and level," Sylvester answered. The tightness in his voice came over the intercom. "They've picked us up on radar, and sent the jets out. Try again to raise Miami. We've got to set up two-way communications."

Then they heard the call in their headsets, and this time they knew at once it was for them: "Amigo Airways Super Connie zero four niner hotel, if you read this transmission turn to and hold a heading of three six zero degrees."

At once Dick Sylvester dropped the right wing fifteen degrees and slowly swung the aircraft around. He kept his eyes fixed on the panel compass and rolled the big plane out of the turn exactly on the heading of magnetic north as he had been directed. That much, at least, he knew he could do right. The jets, as though fastened in position by some invisible means, stayed in the exact relative positions they had first taken off the left wingtip.

"Now what do we do?" Ed Chang realized he was repeating himself, but he couldn't help it.

"Nothing. They'll tell us." Sylvester's voice was flat, as though he had been caught in some unforgivable crime. The ball was no longer in his hands.

"Amigo zero four niner hotel, this is Miami radar. Observed your turn to three six zero degrees. Maintain present heading and hold your transponder inoperative. Remain this frequency. Stand by for ATC clearance."

Chang had a sudden thought. He reached over to the VHF set and put it on the emergency frequency, 121.5. Then he picked up the microphone and spoke: "Air Force one zero two interceptor, this is Amigo Connie four niner hotel. Do you read me?"

The answer came almost at once, but not from the aircraft

to which it was addressed. "Amigo zero four niner hotel, this is Miami Oceanic Control. Go ahead."

Dick Sylvester made a quick gesture that he wanted to talk. He took his own microphone from the clip and spoke into it. "Miami Control, this is Amigo four niner hotel. I wish to close a flight plan. Do you read me?"

"Amigo four niner hotel, read you four square. Proceed with your flight plan."

"Miami control, four niner hotel. I wish to close a flight plan for Civil Air Patrol L six tail number six six seven. Aircraft made emergency landing at Tres Santos airport. Could not close flight plan sooner because no communications. Land line telephone out. Aircraft slightly damaged on landing, crew uninjured and safe."

The answer was crisp and immediate. "Four niner hotel. Understand you are closing flight plan for CAP six six seven. Pilot made emergency landing at Tres Santos. Plane damaged but crew safe and uninjured. Please stand by."

The panel clock measured off the seconds while other messages flooded the frequency. The Connie flew on steadily, the turbulence for the moment behind her.

"Amigo four niner hotel, CAP six six seven flight plan closed. All search aircraft monitoring this frequency, mission is canceled, return to base. Four niner hotel stand by."

Dick Sylvester stole a look out the side window—the jets were still there. He knew they meant big trouble and his muscles tensed.

"Amigo four niner hotel, this is Miami radar. Request point of departure, route of flight, pilot's name, persons on board, fuel remaining, and pilot's intentions."

That was better; the strength of communications took them out of the limbo they had been in. Sylvester felt more confident now as he answered. "Miami radar, this is four niner hotel. Departed Tres Santos direct Victor Foxtrot Romeo to Miami International. Estimate fuel remaining three five hundred gallons. Pilot's name . . ." He took a deep breath. ". . . Sylvester."

A different voice cut in as soon as he had finished. "Amigo four niner hotel, stand by for ATC clearance."

The first voice returned at once. "Amigo four niner hotel, advise persons on board."

Chang picked up his mike and chopped his left hand horizontally through the air to indicate that he would speak. Sylvester looked at him, confusion on his face. "Miami radar from four niner hotel," Ed said clearly. "Persons on board, two crew, seventy-eight passengers."

It was out now. He glanced over at Sylvester, who was staring at him in stark disbelief.

"Four niner hotel, read you seventy-eight pax, how many crew?"

"Repeat, two crew."

It got no further. Another voice came on and took over the frequency. "Amigo Connie four niner hotel, here is your ATC clearance. From present position, direct Nassau. Fifty-two Victor Biscayne. Direct Miami VORTAC, to descend to and maintain eight thousand. Cross Nassau at eight thousand, report Christie intersection and report established inbound on one zero seven radial of Nassau VOR."

The hands with which Captain Sylvester gripped the wheels of the Constellation were white from the rigid pressure of his fingers. His face was locked into a mask of shock and frightened despair. For a few seconds Chang thought that his partner had lost control of himself. Then Sylvester spoke, and the voice was not his own.

"How many passengers?"

"Seventy-eight." It was not a time to explain. "Did you understand the clearance?"

The shock would not lift; Sylvester spoke mechanically. "We have to descend to eight thousand and go to Nassau. We should be almost there now. The rest was completely over my head. Did you understand?"

"No, I can't fly instruments."

Sylvester turned his head, the same expression still frozen on his features. "I can't go on," he said. "I can't believe it. I don't understand it. I don't know what to do."

He wrenched his hands from the control wheel and buried his face in them in a desperate attempt to shut out the world.

Chapter Nine /

ED CHANG TOOK A QUICK FIRM GRIP ON THE control yoke with his right hand and rested his left carefully on the trim tab wheel. His own mind was churning, but the thoughts separated themselves out into rapid, sharp flashes. The passengers—he could not help their being on board. He had done right to withhold the fact from Dick; if Dick had known he might never have made the take-off. The jets— they were the Law, but they were also a possible help if he could talk to them. He had called them on the standard emergency frequency, but they had not replied. Then he remembered reading somewhere that they carried UHF equipment only, so that was that.

He corrected a small bump and turned the yoke to bring

the wings back into level attitude. Sylvester was still sitting motionless in the left-hand seat, apparently oblivious of what was going on in the cockpit.

At that moment Chang grew completely calm and consciously braced his narrow shoulders. It was now up to him. He, Lieutenant Edmund Chang, would take over. He would fly the plane to Miami and he would put it on the runway there just as well as he had put down the little light planes in which he had learned to fly. He would come in faster, and flare higher, but he was getting the feel of the big aircraft. He could not return to the flight engineer's station, but that was no matter.

Carefully he looked at the center control pedestal and verified the fact that there was a set of throttles and handles for the gear and flaps. That would do it; to hell with the other refinements and systems which were not essential to the operation of the aircraft. With power, the landing gear, and the wing flaps, he was in business. He checked the rudder pedals and found that the co-pilot too had a set of brakes. That was important. Without brakes to slow down and stop the landing roll there could be trouble. He knew that the propellers could reverse, but he did not know how to make them do so. There was no time now to read the manual.

He was deeply, and in a way profoundly, grateful for the opportunity which fate had pushed into his hands. Ever since he had left Hawaii he had to fight the battle of his heritage, the fact that his features classed him with the Asiatic peoples. There were even some who were not quite willing to consider him an American. Now he had a chance to prove the worth not so much of himself as of the whole great group of Chinese-Americans to which he belonged.

By doing something which had to be recognized as good, he could justify himself and all the others like him. He could help to underline the injustice of the oriental exclusion immigration laws, he could add a small bit to the sum total of Chinese-American prestige, and he could add honor to the memory of his forebears. After he had safely landed the Constellation, no one at the airport would call him a Chink. They would call him "Lieutenant," and if he reflected enough credit too on the Civil Air Patrol, before long it might even be "Captain."

Then he remembered the complex flight plan which he had not acknowledged. With a quiet confidence which fitted his new role he picked up the microphone, waited for a break on the frequency, and reported in.

"Miami Control, this is Amigo four niner hotel. Negative on ATC clearance, pilot qualified for Victor Foxtrot Romeo only. Will follow all instructions regarding heading and altitude, now descending to eight thousand as directed. Request Victor Foxtrot Romeo landing Miami International."

The headset came alive crisply. "Four niner hotel stand by."

Chang rolled the horizontal trim tab forward slightly and watched the vertical speed indicator. The needle sank to a position which showed a rate of descent of two hundred feet per minute. That was fine. He watched the altimeter unwind slowly and made it a point of pride to attempt to roll the trim tab back and level off at exactly eight thousand feet. He missed by fifty feet and climbed back up again. Then he remembered he was cleared to fly to Nassau; he guessed at a heading of 305 degrees and turned the plane to the left. Like twin specters of disaster, the delta-winged jets went with him and did not leave their relative positions for a moment.

He heard himself called in the headset. "Amigo four niner hotel, this is Miami radar. Disregard all previous transmissions. Expect interception by Air Rescue C one thirty and escort to Homestead Air Force Base. Report escort aircraft in sight. Homestead weather is Victor Foxtrot Romeo, wind southeast twelve knots, altimeter two niner eight six."

"Wilco four niner hotel."

The communication brought an unexpected blessing. In less than twenty seconds the jet interceptors pulled up their flaps and gear, poised for a second in the sky, and then spurted ahead and away. In less than a minute they were out of sight.

Robert Galloway had finished his meal, but his appetite was not entirely satisfied. He decided to indulge himself in another piece of chocolate cream pie. "How about you guys?" he asked the others. "Anybody join me?"

Scotty Zimmerman shook his head. "I'll just have another coffee."

Before Herb Stallings could say anything the PA system stopped their conversation abruptly. "Your attention, please," it came on. "Will anyone from Amigo Airways now in the terminal please answer the paging phone. Will anyone from Amigo Airways . . ."

"I'll take it," Scotty offered. "They probably want us to move Lizzie."

Something in Galloway's inner consciousness told him this was not the case, but he let it ride. Scotty left the table and picked up the convenient phone near to the cashier's desk. He spoke only briefly, then he waved his arm in the air to indicate that the others were to come.

"They want us," Sims said. Galloway picked up the check

quickly, certain now that his first hunch had been right. Zimmerman met him and Sims and Wilson halfway to the exit.

"We're needed at Air Traffic Control. Something's up," he said tersely.

Galloway stopped long enough to pay the bill, then he joined the others who were waiting for him. They went upstairs to the traffic section where the chief controller on duty was waiting for them just inside the doorway. As they gathered around him, he began, "Who's Sylvester?"

"I don't know any Sylvester," Galloway answered quickly. "First or last name?"

"Last I think. You should know him—zero four niner hotel is your Connie, isn't it?"

"That's right," Stallings answered. "It's sitting at Tres Santos tied down against the blow."

"The hell it is! It's approaching Nassau right now at eight thousand feet."

"That's impossible!" Toolie Sims burst out.

The chief controller withered him with a look. "When we first picked it up on radar it wasn't squawking, but that could have been a transponder out without the crew's knowledge. When the aircraft didn't answer a sequence of radio calls we notified the Guard and they scrambled two F-102's to go out and take a look. They reported that it was your Connie all right and verified the tail number."

Despite his dark skin Toolie Sims actually seemed to grow pale. Herb Stallings remained silent, waiting to hear the rest.

"As soon as we had two-way communication we asked all the usual questions. The pilot's name is Sylvester: he reported plenty of fuel, seventy-eight pax on board and, get this, a crew of only two."

"Seventy eight pax," Stallings repeated. "Where from?"

"We don't know. We also don't know how a Connie ever took off with a crew of two, but that isn't the worst of it."

"Go on," Galloway said.

"Since the pilot gave Miami International as his destination, we sent him a clearance."

"I'm going to meet him," Galloway stated.

"Wait a minute; it isn't that simple."

"You're damn right it isn't," Stallings added.

"What do you mean?" the chief controller asked.

"I'll tell you after you finish. Go on."

"All right, now get this: after we fed the pilot his clearance he came back and turned it down on the grounds *that he wasn't qualified to fly instruments!*"

"That's fantastic!" Wilson said. Since the comment was totally unnecessary, no one paid any attention to it.

"Then he asked for a contact clearance in. That's when I sent for you. I remembered that one of your threes came in a little while ago."

Of all of the men present Herb Stallings was the one who kept his head the most. "I don't know Sylvester," he began, "and I can't imagine why he's got the Connie—not the faintest idea—but I think I can explain part of this. We left the Connie at Tres Santos because she was red-lined, complete failure of the hydraulic elevator boost system. With boost out she's unsafe, and illegal, to fly. The pax is puzzling though. Can't figure that. Unless he's collected everyone in the neighborhood." He shook his head. "If Sylvester, whoever he is, took off and then found the elevator boost out, he might refuse an instrument clearance on those grounds."

"Then he would have said so," the chief controller disagreed. "He specifically reported that he was *not qualified* to fly instruments. If he found boost out he could have declared an emergency, and should have."

"Possibly he failed his last check and was sticking by the book," Zimmerman suggested.

"Then if he had a brain in his head he would have taken the clearance anyway and explained when he got here. He sure as hell wouldn't try to come barging in, under the conditions we have now, with a VFR clearance."

There was no answer for that, and there was silence for a few seconds. Then Galloway spoke. "When is he due in?"

"He isn't. Taking him at his word we notified Air Rescue. They have a C-130 out to intercept him and lead him through the traffic to Homestead."

"I want to know who Sylvester is," Galloway said. "He had absolutely no authority to move that aircraft and the log book is clearly red-lined. I verified it myself."

For answer the chief controller led the way inside. He stopped at the end of the long row of air traffic control stations and spoke to the man on duty. "Raise Connie four niner hotel and ask the pilot for his full ID."

The duty man nodded and spoke into his microphone. The seconds ticked away as he waited for and received his answer.

"Pilot is Captain Richard Sylvester, Civil Air Patrol. Co-pilot and engineer is Lieutenant Edmund Chang, also CAP."

The chief controller's eyes suddenly hardened and focused on something an infinite distance away. "My God," he said softly.

He did not wait to explain. He reached for a phone in the row of several and gave a quick order. "Get me the CAP group commander immediately."

There was a thick silence while he waited for the connection.

"CAP, Colonel Williams," came over the line.

"Colonel, this is Miami Air Traffic Control. Who were the two pilots who were overdue on their flight plan this morning?"

"Captain Dick Sylvester, Lieutenant Edmund Chang, that's C-h-a-n-g."

The chief controller took a quick breath. "Can you tell me without looking it up if either of them is qualified on a ten forty niner Super-Constellation?"

"They're not, positively. They're both good in single-engine light aircraft, but that's all."

"Instrument qualified, either of them?"

"Negative."

"All right, Colonel, the facts are these: we have an inbound Super Connie with seventy-eight passengers aboard. Your boys are flying it."

"Alone?"

"Apparently so. Furthermore, the plane was taken without permission and is red-lined in an unsafe condition."

The CAP commander's voice seemed somewhat strained. "I can't explain it, but both men are normally reliable. Sylvester has a secret clearance. To the best of my knowledge neither of them has any multi-engine experience whatever. What's the red line?"

"Elevator boost failure."

"You'd better get out the crash equipment and the meat wagon. How about Homestead?"

"Affirmative, they're being intercepted and led in there by an Air Rescue C-130."

"I'll go over there immediately. If you need me I'll be airborne in about five minutes."

"Right, Colonel, thank you."

The chief controller replaced the phone. "This is a helluva mess. We've had to alert Homestead and prepare them for an emergency. We've also notified the state police, the Customs Service, the Immigration Service, the AP's, and the FBI. Add to that Air Rescue and the Air Guard who sent out the interceptors with orders to shoot your bird down if the pilot made one false move. You know why. Now the CAP is in on it, we are, and so are you."

"I want to go over there immediately," Galloway said. "Can you get me permission to land there in a three?"

"Get going, I'll call you in flight. I'm sure that under the circumstances they'll let you in."

His face grim, Galloway hurriedly led the way out of the room.

Lieutenant Colonel Raymond Williams hung up the phone with considerably less confidence than he had put into his conversation. It was his unfailing rule to back his men up publicly if at all possible and give them hell, if they needed it, privately at a later time. Now the very pretty girl who had been sitting in the corner of his office was on her feet imploring his attention.

"Tell me, please!" she pleaded.

The colonel started to take the easy way out. "Lieutenant Chang is aboard an inbound Connie from Tres Santos. He should be landing at Homestead Air Force Base within the hour." When he had said that much he realized he was being grossly unfair; he had better prepare her for what lay ahead. "Miss Wong, I've got to add something to that. I don't have all the facts yet, but apparently your friend and his companion have helped themselves to a four-engine Constellation airliner and are flying it up here with a large load of passengers."

He looked her squarely in the eye and judged that she could take it. "The fact is, they aren't qualified to fly that airplane—they don't even come close. I don't know why or how they got it off the ground, but getting it back on is going to be one whale of a problem for them. I'm going over to Homestead now; if you'd like, I'll phone you when they have landed."

"Please, no," Doris answered quickly. "I want to come with you." Her voice caught. "I've *got* to. Please take me!"

Colonel Williams had anticipated that. He opened his mouth to refuse, and then thought again. "If I take you, after we land you'll have to keep quiet and not mention to anyone that you're not a CAP member."

"But I am," Doris interrupted. "That is, I just filed my application. Ed wants me to learn flying too."

"We don't teach flying, but never mind that now. Come along."

Six minutes later Colonel Williams was airborne in his personal Cessna 310 twin. With him he had his executive and operations officers and a highly distraught Miss Doris Wong. As he retracted the gear for the short flight to Homestead Air Force Base he reflected that the idiot who had first said that oriental peoples never show any emotion on their faces should be with him now.

Brigadier General Scott Ayms, Commander, Homestead Air Force Base, listened intently to the briefing he was receiving from *his* operations officer.

"That about sums it up, sir," the major concluded. "For reasons not yet known these two young men took the C-121G and left Tres Santos with a considerable load of pax. CAP confirms that they have no multi-engine experience, have never flown anything but light aircraft, and are not instrument qualified."

"We may have to shoot them down to get them on the ground," the general commented. "Then what we have, Ben, is a civilian C-121G full of warm bodies flown by two amateur pilots who have never handled or landed an aircraft of that size."

"And with a primary control system inoperative, yes, sir."

"Well, it won't help them to have us sit here and talk about it. First, alert all emergency facilities including the base hospital. I want a medical officer and all necessary support on the spot when that Connie comes in. Also arrange to have the HH-43B chopper orbiting and ready with the fire suppression kit at least five minutes before the ETA."

"Yes, sir. That's already been done, sir."

"Good. Then check the alert crews and see if we can lay our hands on a pilot who is C-121 qualified. He doesn't have to be current, just as long as he is familiar with the bird. At the same time check the club, and quarters if necessary; get the best man you can locate in a hurry."

"Right."

"Meanwhile put a T-bird on the line ready for immediate take-off. As soon as you have your man, put him in the back seat. You know the rest."

"Yes, sir, they're to intercept the C-121 and talk the pilot down."

The general was thinking rapidly. "I don't know anything about those passengers. Notify the immigration and customs services what we have coming in. Alert the AP's and have them inform the FBI. This is in their area too, of course. Also put in a courtesy call to the state police; they may want to be on hand."

"Yes, sir." The major knew that most of this had already been done, but he also knew better than to interrupt the general with unnecessary comments.

"Get hold of the chaplain and brief him. The people riding with those lunatics may be half out of their minds. The Lord only knows what's going on in that airplane."

"Two quick items, sir. The owner of the Constellation is en route from Miami International in a C-47 and requests permission to land. It's a civilian bird."

"O.K."

"Colonel Williams, the group CAP commander, will arrive shortly with his exec and ops man. They're in a civilian U-3A with CAP authorization."

"Good. Alert me personally about ten minutes before the C-121 is due. Also I want to know when, as, and if we have a C-121 qualified pilot on the scene and in two-way communication with whoever is flying that Connie. Better keep me posted all along the line."

"Right, sir." The operations officer had a lot to do in very little time. He left as abruptly as he could and almost leaped for the nearest telephone.

Dick Sylvester realized that, whether he liked it or not, he was, in effect, the commander of an over-ocean international airliner flight with a full load of passengers and a first-class emergency situation on his hands. Furthermore the time of decision was coming closer. In a few minutes Nassau should be in sight; from there on into Miami would be a short trip. After that, the landing.

He sat still for a moment and gathered himself together. Then he aligned in his mind the things which had caused him to feel so engulfed.

First, there had been the jets. They were expensive to fly and there was no doubt that they had been scrambled because of him.

Secondly, there had been the complicated instrument clearance which he had not understood and which he was powerless to follow. Then, to cap it all off, there had been the news of his incredible load of passengers. He had believed himself to be carrying three people, two in urgent need of medical care and a third to look after and comfort them. He had no idea where all those other people had come from and right now he didn't care. First he would deliver them safely on the ground; after that he would want a lot of questions answered.

As he assembled the things which had caused his breakup, he began to look each of them in the face more calmly. The jets were gone. There might be some hell about that later, but for the present that problem, at least, was solved.

Next, the clearance. He had clearly heard the instructions to disregard it. A C-130 from the Air Rescue Service was coming to help them. That would solve all navigational problems and he might even be given a little useful advice along the way. Although it was a turboprop, the C-130 was also a four-engined aircraft and the pilot could probably help him a lot.

That left the problem of the passengers. Well, a Connie was a Connie and perhaps it flew better with at least a partial load than if it was empty. The critical point with a big load was always the take-off, and that was well behind them. By the time they reached Miami they would probably have burned off enough gas to more than make up for the added weight, if not—so what. A Connie wasn't a baby carriage—it was intended to haul people in wholesale quantities. His responsibility was increased, but that was all. Quite possibly the big bird would stick on the runway better with some ballast on board. Empty she might have a tendency to float halfway down the field and that could lead to real trouble.

To give himself something to do he checked his seat belt, then fussed with the adjustment of the rudder pedals and the pilot's chair. After that he surveyed the instruments and read those he could understand. The sound of the engines was good; Ed had done a fine job there; they were even quieter, which meant that his partner had them synchronized after a fashion.

What the hell, he had landed airplanes hundreds of times. Little light ones, of course, but a bird was a bird. He would have to come in a lot faster, but on the other hand he would have a beautiful, long, paved runway. His lips began to twist into a tight little ghost of a smile. He would taxi in. He saw himself doing that, properly behind the "Follow Me" jeep, and with something new and damn important to put into his log book.

How many guys were there anyway who flew four-engined airplanes every day? Hundreds! It was about time he joined the fraternity. Six hundred hours plus was a good pile of time and he knew all about stall speeds, glides, flares, cross-winds if he got stuck with one, and stuff like that. All of the values would be different in a Connie, of course, but he could feel if she was near the stall, he was pretty confident of that. If he brought her over the fence at 150 indicated, that ought to be all right. After he chopped the power she would slow up mighty fast and come on.

He reached up and took hold of the control yoke. "Thanks, Ed," he said into the intercom. "It got me for a minute, but I'm all right now."

Chang looked over and grinned at him. "I don't blame you," he came back. "Now let's get this bird to Nassau and pick up our escort. This is going to be a big day in the history of the CAP."

"I hope so. I heard we're supposed to land at Homestead."

"That's right, and an ARS C one thirty is going to lead us in."

Sylvester thought a minute and then asked, "Ed, with the elevator boost out we've got a pretty fair problem on our hands. Do you think I should call in and declare an emergency?"

Chang had a ready answer, but he pretended to ponder the matter for a moment. "I don't think so, at least not right now. Those jets got to me too. As I see it, the less attention we draw to ourselves on this flight, the better."

"I'm with you on that," Sylvester agreed. "If we get them all shook up down there it could complicate matters considerably."

"Why don't we do it this way," Chang suggested. "When the C-130 gets here I'll try to talk to the pilot on 121.5. Since it's a rescue aircraft, I'm positive we can communicate. I'll advise him we have a mechanical problem, but that so far we have it licked."

"Good, I'll buy that. Then when we're about five minutes out or so call the tower at Homestead, tell them who we are, and ask permission to land. Better add to that that we have two people on board in urgent need of medical attention. At an air base they'll have facilities available and probably a doctor on duty."

"If not they can get hold of one mighty fast. Also there'll be an ambulance on or near the line."

"Right, with the hot stuff they fly, that's probably SOP."

"I think it's a lot smarter that way," Chang said.

Dick Sylvester felt materially better. "I think we're on top of this thing now, Ed. The more we think of it as routine, the better chance we have to make it just that."

"Your ki is flowing. You don't know what that means, but what it amounts to is that you are master of yourself. That's Buddha-head philosophy, but believe me, it works."

Dick Sylvester allowed the little smile which had been fighting for life to be born. His face relaxed and he turned toward his partner with real confidence in his eyes.

"O.K., then, we play it cool. We'll just fly over to Homestead, get into the pattern, and then tell them we're on the way. Five minutes' notice is all they'll need. We might even be number one to land. If they're sticky about it, I'll tell them we have medical patients who must have attention and declare an emergency on that basis."

"Fine," Chang responded. "That's one hundred percent kosher all the way. They may have to get a doctor down to the flight line, but we need him anyway—pretty badly I should think. You fly, I'll handle the engines, gear, flaps, and the communications."

Now the modest little smile broadened into one of strength and determination. "You know what, Ed? After we're on the ground and all this is behind us, let's report to Colonel Williams together. After all, we're in the life-saving business, and won't we have something to tell him!"

Chapter Ten /

THE WIND, WHICH WAS THE BEGINNING
fringe of Hurricane Hazel, mounted rapidly in intensity at
Tres Santos airport until the already angry waters at the
shoreline began to rage and the few palm trees around the
small terminal bent almost to their elastic limit. The metal
hangar crackled heavily under the buffeting, fighting to hold
itself together in the face of ever-mounting forces. The
windicator swung back and forth in short jerky arcs as it
tried desperately to keep up with the vagaries of the sharp
gusts which quartered the deserted runway. As the sounds
of the coming storm mounted, they echoed across a deserted
field with no human ears to hear them and interpret their
meaning.

In moderate to heavy turbulence, Captain Ned Arjarian, USAF, piloting his Air Rescue Service RC-54 *Rescuemaster* by hand, arrived over the field at two thousand feet and began to make a visual survey of the situation below. With more than five thousand hours to his credit, Captain Arjarian knew the score as he knew the veteran four-engine, piston-powered, unpressurized aircraft he was flying. After six solid years in the ARS he was thoroughly accustomed to flying in vile weather of every sort and kind. Within its known limitations he had complete confidence in his bird and even more so in its select crew under his command. Although it was rugged duty at times, the prime mission of saving human lives, regardless of whose they were, appealed to him enormously. Evacuating civilian personnel in the path of destructive hurricanes was right up his alley.

Swinging the RC-54 in a lazy circle to the left he made a detailed study of the ground area below him. He spotted the small cluster of fragile-looking, boxlike dwellings situated in the trees a mile from the airport and correctly deduced that they were the homes of the airport workers and their dependents. He saw no signs of human life, but that meant little—what people there were below would be inside against the anger of the wind. They could not be aware that the plane they heard overhead, if they did, had been sent specifically to airlift them to a place of greater safety. The Air Rescue Service came all too seldom because its equipment was limited, its mission colossal, and most of its people were already working a ninety-hour week.

As he completed his inspection of the ground area Captain Arjarian called the Tres Santos tower. When no reply came after several seconds he tried once more as a formality. The lack of any answer did not surprise him; normal operations would be suspended in the face of the oncoming hurricane and he had expected that the tower would be secured. A careful visual check of the area showed no hint of any other traffic. Satisfied that he was alone in that immediate part of the sky, he called for twenty degrees of flap and lined up the runway for a landing.

"Gear down," he ordered.

"Gear down." His co-pilot leaned forward and looked down and ahead at the windicator. "Mighty tough crosswind, Ned," he advised. "It looks well over the allowable factor." He spoke because Arjarian was the kind of aircraft commander who wanted to see all of his crew members using their heads all of the time.

"What crosswind?" Arjarian asked dryly.

"Just look at the tet, there on the left-hand side!"

"What crosswind?" the captain repeated.

The co-pilot awoke and saw the light. "I beg your pardon, captain, I just looked again. It's right down the runway."

"Fine. We've got an estimated eighty people to pick up and I'd hate to disappoint them."

The co-pilot checked the panel. "Gear down and locked."

Arjarian concentrated completely on his approach; he was flying by eye reference to the ground and by the seat of his pants with no time to spare to look at the gauges. His co-pilot tried to relax and look indifferent, but failed completely because he was aware that he was more than a little scared. He knew Arjarian was good, damn good, but the best pilot alive couldn't handle a heavy crosswind far above allowable vectors, and what they were flying into was just that. There was only one runway and there was no other field on the island.

"No more flap, Joe," Arjarian said, looking straight ahead

and almost without moving his lips. "I'm going to put her on fast and cut down the wind component."

The co-pilot answered by tightening his seat belt.

The RC-54 came over the end of the runway in a crab and flared. Arjarian waited for the right moment to kick her straight with the rudder just before she paid off, but the crab angle close to the ground told him he would never make it with any degree of safety. The engineer was ready with his hands poised above the throttles.

"Maximum power."

"Maximum power." The engineer pushed the levers forward as fast as the engines could respond and took a deep breath when the landing successfully aborted and the propellers in low pitch pulled the aircraft back up to safety.

Ned Arjarian was still climbing out straight ahead when he felt a tap on his shoulder. He looked back to see Sergeant Greg Harris claiming his attention. "Request permission to jump," the sergeant said.

The captain thought about it. Harris was a man who never ceased to amaze him; he seemed to have a limitless capacity to do anything. He was one of the hundred and sixty odd pararescuemen in the service who, by their own creed, are ready and willing to jump anywhere, at any time, under any conditions, to rescue anyone. Harris was more than a parachutist—he was an expert SCUBA diver, a highly-qualified medical technician, a survival specialist, and several things more.

"Pretty heavy wind," Arjarian hedged.

"That's all right, sir. I've gone out in worse."

"You might have to sit out the blow down there. Unless we get a break in the wind, a landing doesn't look too good.

Of course if we have to do it to save those people, we will."

Harris actually grinned under his tight crew cut. "Sir, do you remember that Greenland rescue attempt last winter? I sat it out for eight days through an arctic ice storm along with Airman Schloeffler. We built an igloo at twenty-eight below and made out just fine."

"I get the point." The aircraft commander turned back toward the island at twelve hundred feet. "Permission granted."

Six minutes later Sergeant Harris went out the door with full medical equipment and an extra ration pack. His chute opened promptly and in a matter of a minute or so he was on the ground. He spilled his canopy expertly, waved quickly that he was fine, and started for the terminal. Arjarian swung in a lazy orbit pattern to await a report; meanwhile he kept an alert watch for any sign of a let-up in the wind or a shift of direction which would increase the chances of a safe landing.

Presently Harris came in on his small portable transceiver. "There's no one around here at all," he reported. "The terminal's unlocked and I checked inside. The land line telephone is out. There is a small L-6 USAF aircraft stored with the wings off in the terminal building, probably against the storm."

"Can you check the village?" Arjarian asked. It was his way of giving an order to a man he genuinely respected.

"Easily. There's an old Chevvy with the key in it here, probably the line car. I'm going to borrow it."

"Go ahead."

Captain Arjarian guided the RC-54 through two more orbits in the rough, unruly air and then Harris came in once more. "Negative on the village; no one there at all. Some other evacuation ship has been in and taken them all away."

"It must have been commercial," Arjarian replied. "Funny they didn't let us know."

"It happens that way sometimes. Captain, I advise strongly against attempting a landing here. The gusts are very strong and are up to sixty percent across the runway."

"Can you make out all right?"

"Affirmative. I've got everything I need and with the terminal building available no sweat. I can sleep late."

Harris was probably right at that. The terminal building was obviously solidly built, Arjarian could tell that from the air, and with good shelter available there should be no problem at all.

"O.K., see you later," he radioed down, and signed off. This done he ordered more power, climbed to nine thousand and called in for a clearance. As soon as he had contact he reported that there had been a prior evacuation flight from Tres Santos and advised that the field was unusable because of prohibitive crosswinds. The information was relayed on by Miami Control and fed to Homestead Air Force Base as a matter of routine.

Major Ben Griffin moved with considerable speed and efficiency. As soon as he had left the general's office he had first alerted the chaplain and had briefed him on the problem. The duty chaplain had at once left his quarters and was on his way to the flight line.

The Public Health Service rang through on the land line telephone and asked if it was true that an unscheduled Connie was coming in with a full load of uncleared, unmanifested passengers. The major confirmed that and told Public Health that the ETA was still open, but the plane was expected within the hour.

Also, in the same ten minutes, he had gotten hold of the right people and had a Lockheed T-33 two-seat jet ordered on the line in the least possible time.

Finally he had called the alert facility and drawn a blank: none of the alert pilots was Connie qualified. They knew a man who was, but a call to his quarters got no answer.

The next best bet was the Officers' Club. Ben dialed the number, waited while the phone rang six times, and then reached the steward. Without wasting time on explanations he asked that the paging system be used to put out an immediate call for anyone, repeat anyone, familiar with and able to fly the C-121G whether or not current in the aircraft.

He waited four agonizing minutes plus a short part of a fifth, then Major Sam Aschenbrenner answered the page from the bar. "What's the C-121 problem?" he asked.

"This is Major Griffin, Operations. How well do you know the bird?"

"I have about three thousand hours in her as A/C," Aschenbrenner answered, "but I haven't flown one for the last four months."

"We need you urgently," Griffin said. "General Ayms asked me to get hold of a Connie pilot as quickly as possible. Can you come down to the flight line immediately, please."

Aschenbrenner's voice became businesslike. "Give me just a minute to excuse myself from my guests and I'm on my way."

"Fine. I'll get a staff car up there for you on the double. You can pick it up outside."

Nine minutes later Major Samuel Aschenbrenner reported

to the flight line in a sports jacket and light-colored slacks suitable for the cocktail hour. Just as he arrived the T-bird taxied up in front of Operations, lit and ready to go. Ben Griffin saw it, signaled to the pilot to indicate he should chop the engine, and motioned him inside.

A young first lieutenant in flight gear responded to the summons. Griffin took the two men inside and spent three and a half minutes in briefing them. When he had finished he allowed himself to savor the expressions on their faces. The T-bird pilot looked slightly petrified; Aschenbrenner was more reflective, weighing the matter in his mind. "You've got a beaut, there's no doubt about that. It would be a pretty good case with a normally functioning aircraft and no load. With a full haul of pax things are more complicated. With a major control system inoperative, it's a real can of worms."

A Cessna 310 light twin taxied up outside of Operations and the fans stopped promptly. Three officers got out and a young woman who, even at a distance, merited attention. They came inside quickly and Griffin went to meet them. On his way out the phone rang; he turned toward the lieutenant and indicated that he was to answer it for him.

Griffin was shaking hands with Colonel Williams when the T-33 pilot punched him on the shoulder. "General Ayms," he said shortly.

Griffin was on the line in twelve seconds. "What progress?" the general wanted to know.

"All the facilities and organizations that you specified are alerted, sir, also the Public Health Service. The duty chaplain is on his way down. Colonel Williams, the CAP group commander, has just arrived with two of his officers and a young woman. I haven't met her yet."

"Have you located a C-121 pilot yet?"

"Yes, sir, I got hold of Major Aschenbrenner at the Officers' Club. He's here now and I've just briefed him."

"Sam Aschenbrenner?" the general said. "We're in luck; he's one of the very best. We flew together ten years ago. Give him my regards."

"I will, sir. The T-bird is ready and Major Aschenbrenner is just about to leave."

"Fine. It might be a good idea to introduce him to Colonel Williams for a moment if that's convenient. You can see why."

"Right, sir, I can. Unless you hear from me to the contrary, Major Aschenbrenner will be airborne and out of here in less than ten minutes."

"Ben, before you go, after you get Sam on his way invite the CAP officers up to my office. Also bring up the owner of the Connie when he comes in. Do you know who it is?"

"Negative, sir, but I'll advise you as soon as he's here."

"Do that." The general hung up.

The conference between Aschenbrenner and Williams was brief. In essence the colonel offered to bet any reasonable amount that there was some element in this thing which had not yet come to light. He knew his boys pretty well and they weren't the reckless kind.

Aschenbrenner in turn asked for a quick sketch of the two men. He listened carefully and approved of the colonel's powers of description.

"I shouldn't have too much trouble talking them down, then?" he asked.

"Definitely not. They're both thoroughly intelligent, conscientious young men really dedicated to flying and the CAP mission. Chang is more the optimist; Sylvester is a little bit on the egghead side—a thinker."

"Sylvester is doing the flying?"

"Both of them are, I'm sure of that, but Sylvester gave his name as pilot when he reported in. That's proper—he's older by a bit, has more time, and is the senior in rank."

"Think he probably started this thing and Chang went along for the ride?"

"No, I don't think so. If anything I would expect Chang to be the first to suggest it. But, knowing them as I do, I'm positive it was a mutual decision and one based on something we still don't know about."

"One last point: how well does Chang speak English?"

The colonel was startled for a moment. "As well as we do. He's an American. Native-born in Hawaii, I think. In fact he's about the most articulate man in my command. I've been considering him for IO."

Aschenbrenner glanced quickly at his watch. "I'll check with you as soon as I get back," he said. "I'll see if I can't get your boys and their passengers down all right. If they make it, I'll buy the first round."

"I will," Williams answered. "Godspeed."

"I'm worried," Chang said.

"Keep your spirits up," Sylvester advised. "We're more than halfway home. We know now we can fly this thing, we've proved it. All we have to do is set it down and I know darn well we can."

The lieutenant shook his head in spite of the headset and the fact that he was, for the moment, handling the controls.

"That isn't it. I'm worried about Doris."

"Why, isn't she all right?"

"As far as I know she is. But I had a date with her this afternoon."

"So what. Call her up and explain after we get in."

Chang reached for the trim tab and made a slight adjustment. Then he looked forward through the windshield and for a moment abruptly changed the subject. "I wish we knew how to use the birddog on this thing. It would be nice to have a needle point right to where we want to go."

"We'll find Nassau," Sylvester asserted. "With Andros and all those other islands out there, we can't miss."

Chang came back to what was really on his mind. "You might as well know this. We've been going together for some time."

"I do know that."

"Well, last night I popped the question."

Sylvester wisely kept still.

"She didn't give me an answer right away," Chang went on. "She promised she would when I came to get her this afternoon."

"You're in." Sylvester did his best to stretch his arms in the rather cramped cockpit. "She wouldn't have made a date with you just to say 'no.' Also, if I know Doris, and I think that I do a little, she won't turn down a good pilot. How soon do you plan on getting married?"

"As soon as she'll have me—if she will," Chang answered. He sighed. "Since we're on the subject, how about yourself?"

Sylvester turned his head and looked out of the left hand side window as though studying the sky. "No traffic so far," he commented, and then returned to the topic. "There was a girl I liked pretty well a while ago. But she didn't like flying and couldn't see me spending my money on lessons instead of on her. So we drifted apart. Nothing much has come up since."

This time Chang nodded his head up and down. "Smart. If she couldn't go you getting something you wanted that much, you're lucky to be out of it."

"Thanks," Sylvester said.

"Will you be my best man?" Chang asked.

The captain looked at him and, for the first time in a long while allowed himself to smile. As he did so the angle of his shoulders relaxed and the tension which held him eased off. "May I kiss the bride?" he asked.

"You'd better."

"Then it's a deal." He looked out through the windshield. "Ed, we've got company. I could be wrong, but that looks like a C-130 out there about eleven o'clock."

Chang leaned over the control yoke and quickly picked up the oncoming aircraft. "A C-130 it is. I like him a lot better than those jets."

"No argument." Sylvester retuned the VHF transceiver to 121.5 and picked up the microphone. "Air Rescue C-130, this is Connie four niner hotel."

The reply almost boomed into his headphones and he had to turn the volume down. "Connie four niner hotel, this is rescue three niner four. Switch to one two two decimal five. If no contact, return this frequency."

"Wilco."

Sylvester tuned the set and was grateful for the number of crystals apparently installed on the airline receiver.

"Rescue three niner four, this is Connie four niner hotel."

"Good, read you five square. Maintain present heading and altitude until we join up. We will take a position slightly ahead of you and to your left."

"The good shepherd," Chang commented.

The big turboprop altered course and swung out in a

sweeping half circle. Chang concentrated on flying as smoothly as he could while the rescue aircraft was maneuvering into position. He had not realized how fast a C-130 was until now.

The radio came on again. "Four niner hotel, understand you have difficulties with your elevator control system."

"Affirmative," Sylvester answered. "Elevator is totally inoperative. We're flying strictly on the horizontal trim tab."

"Also understand you have two crew only, and not qualified on instruments."

That caused Sylvester to tighten up once more. Apparently everybody knew all about them, and it was publicity he would have much preferred to avoid. He answered a little tersely. "Affirmative, pilot and co-pilot not instrument qualified, but we are accustomed to artificial horizon and basic flight instruments. We can follow you through clouds if necessary."

"Negative, not required."

Sylvester decided to take the initiative. "We are also not qualified this aircraft although we are rated CAP pilots. Can you help us?"

There was a short pause. "Four niner hotel, will do the best we can, but no one here qualified in your aircraft. Stand by."

On the new frequency the headphones remained quiet until outside the left window the big Hercules appeared alarmingly close. It pulled ahead a hundred feet or so and took up position well to the left of the Connie wingtip.

"Four niner hotel, will you be able to maintain relative position with us?"

The muscles tightened in Dick Sylvester's jaw. "We can try," he answered. They would darn well find out if they could maintain position. He had told them that he and

Chang were rated pilots. Furthermore, Ed was flying perfectly at the moment; no pro could do any better.

"Four niner hotel, we will lead you in to Homestead Air Force Base."

"Thanks." He knew he should be grateful, but somehow, despite the distortions characteristic of most aircraft communications sets, he felt a stiffness on the part of whoever was doing the talking in the C-130, probably the A/C.

"Dick, will you take over," Chang asked through the intercom. Sylvester was a little surprised by the request and also by the tone of the words. Ed definitely had something on his mind. In response Sylvester raised his hands and took hold of the yoke. Then he remembered and dropped his right hand down onto the trim tab control.

Chang, with a peculiarly cool look on his face, picked up the microphone. "Rescue three niner four."

"Go ahead."

"Can you establish communications with Homestead for us?"

"Affirmative, what is your message?"

"Please advise Homestead to have a medical officer meet us if possible. Also an ambulance." He kept all emotion out of his voice, and his face was a firm mask.

The reply came swiftly, with concern evident in the voice. "Four niner hotel, are you ill? Please advise."

Ed Chang's narrow eyes were half closed; the corners of his mouth were tight. "Negative, crew is O.K. But we have two patients on board in urgent need of medical attention. This flight is being made under emergency conditions for that reason."

Sylvester looked sharply at him—they had agreed not to discuss that.

"Four niner hotel, stand by."

Sylvester contented himself with flying; he could ask his questions later. He looked ahead and felt a sudden sharp emotion. There only a few miles ahead, lay the first of the Bahama Islands, he could not tell which one.

They were still talking to Chang. "Four niner hotel, Homestead will supply doctor and ambulance. They request nature of illness on board and if contagious."

Chang answered very deliberately and with particular articulation in his words. "Negative on contagion. Patient one is a young man, age about twenty-two, with severe abdominal pains believed to be appendicitis. His condition is getting worse. Abdomen is enlarged. Do you read?"

"Affirmative, continue."

"Patient two is a small girl, age about eight. She suffered severe burns this morning when her clothing caught fire. She was given one dose of morphine; no more is available."

The C-130 took time to relay the information and get an acknowledgment.

"Connie four niner hotel, understand yours is a mercy flight, is that correct?"

Knowing that a little more trouble could hardly hurt him now, Ed Chang deliberately violated the strict regulations of the Federal Communications Commission. *"You're damn right it is!"* he replied.

Chapter Eleven /

ALTHOUGH IT WAS LATE ON SUNDAY AFTER-
noon, Brigadier General Scott Ayms was in class A uniform.
It was his contention that a commander at his level of responsibility is never off duty; he was, therefore, in his office
over the weekend more often than not, and usually in uniform. As he sat behind his desk he looked at the assortment
of visitors he had and inwardly prayed that the thing which
had brought them all together would not end in tragedy.

Colonel Williams of the Civil Air Patrol might be a civilian
behind his uniform, he thought, but he certainly knew how
to conduct himself as an officer, and a fairly high-ranking
one at that. The two other CAP men who had come with
him largely kept quiet. Under the circumstances that was

definitely a mark in their favor. The slim Chinese girl sat close by at the general's left. The general had been married almost thirty years, but that did not mean he had been struck blind. He had carefully arranged things to put the girl where she was, partly for his own satisfaction and more practically so he could give her the moral support she was going to need, and possibly need badly.

He liked Galloway, the owner of the hi-jacked airliner, and most of the people with him. He recognized Stallings as a professional and concerning Sims thought that the little operation was exceptionally broad-minded to have a Negro crew member in a highly responsible job. The others were largely just faces, he would take a reading on them later if he felt it necessary to do so.

The phone rang. The general picked it up and said, "Yes?" He listened with a face which revealed no clue as to what he was hearing, or whether it was good news or bad.

"Keep me informed," he directed and replaced the instrument again with no visible emotion.

He looked at his guests. "There's been a small development," he announced, glanced at the girl and added, "On the plus side, I would say."

Doris Wong leaned forward and looked at him, prepared to hear the news. Colonel Williams did not react visibly. Robert Galloway lifted his eyebrows in interrogation. The feeling of tension hung in the air like a thick fog.

"They're almost at Nassau and apparently so far, so good," the general reported. "The Rescue Service C-130 has joined up with them and has set up two-way communication. They seem to be flying the airplane all right." He paused to let it sink in.

"If they haven't ruined the engines or something like that," Wilson interjected.

The general gave him a look that made him regret his own birth.

"I rather doubt that," the general continued calmly. "The C-130 crew is pretty sharp; they have to be. Their flight engineer reports that the C-121, I beg your pardon, the Connie, seems to be in very good shape. They have the gear and flaps up as they should and the cowl flaps are open about thirty degrees."

Toolie Sims noted again the command pilot's wings embroidered on the general's uniform, and picked up the cue. "I would say that was exactly right, sir. Perhaps they know a lot more about the bird than we realize."

The general knew now that Sims was an intelligent man. "They have probably been reading the flight manual, but it's clear they know how to take care of themselves." This time Wilson had sense enough to keep quiet.

"I'm glad to hear that," Galloway said. "My first thought is for them and the passengers, of course. After that, I'm a little concerned for my aircraft."

"Obviously," Ayms said, still in an even, quiet voice, "but with Sam Aschenbrenner out there to talk them in I don't think it is any serious problem." That was strictly a lie, for the benefit of Doris Wong. He turned to her.

"How well do you know the lieutenant?" he asked with exactly the proper amount of polite interest in his voice.

"We're going to be married," Doris answered. The general liked the way she looked at him when she answered.

"The only thing that really baffles me is why they did it," Herb Stallings said. "From what I've heard of them in the last few minutes it's certainly not a prank or anything as far-fetched as that."

"No, it isn't," the general answered slowly. "I have some news on that. About five minutes ago they asked that a doctor and an ambulance meet them at the flight line."

Doris Wong visibly tightened in her chair.

"They report two patients on board in urgent need of medical attention," Ayms continued a little more quickly. "They have a young man with acute appendicitis who apparently needs surgery very promptly and a little girl who was badly burned in a fire."

Colonel Williams of the Civil Air Patrol spoke for the first time. "I knew, sir, there had to be something. Chang and Sylvester are too reliable to have done what they did without an excellent reason. I'm assuming there was no doctor available on the island."

"That's right, no doctor," Scotty Zimmerman confirmed. "We keep a first-aid kit in the terminal, but that's the limit of the normal facilities. I don't know where they got the morphine; our birds don't carry it."

"I'll give them points for the two emergency cases," the general conceded. "That leaves seventy-six more passengers to be accounted for."

The phone rang again, once, discreetly. The general picked it up, acknowledged, and listened. Then he hung up, again with no visible emotion.

"That was Air Rescue," he reported. "They sent a C-54 to Tres Santos to evacuate the personnel. They try to do that whenever a dangerous hurricane is on the loose if they have any suitable equipment in the area. Unfortunately they're spread much too thin and can't possibly take care of everybody. This time they found the place deserted and the little community close by was empty as well."

He looked around, but nobody stated the obvious. "The rescue plane attempted a landing," the general went on, "but aborted because of excessive crosswinds far above the allowable factor. The crew included a pararescueman who jumped and reported from the ground that the place had indeed been cleaned out."

"How did they pick him up?" Galloway asked.

"They didn't. He'll have to sit it out down there until they can get a plane in to retrieve him."

He turned in his chair a few degrees and faced Colonel Williams. "Anyway, Colonel, your boys can show some reason for their actions. That may be of considerable importance when they get here."

Ed Chang reached over to the throttles of the Super-Constellation and made a slight adjustment. He knew there was a synchronization indicator at the flight engineer's station, but he did not want to leave the co-pilot's position to read it. Instead he resynchronized by ear and did a creditable job of it.

When he was through he spoke again through the intercom. "I think it's about time we stopped kidding ourselves, Dick," he said more calmly than he felt. "We've reported to Miami Control that we're flying this bird without instrument tickets. They've sent out jets to look us over. Now we have Air Rescue leading us in. They know how many passengers we have. We've been diverted to a different destination. Add it up—we're not going to sneak quietly into Homestead, land, and then go home. They're waiting for us. See you in jail."

Sylvester took his time. He looked out again at the four-engine rescue craft and then made an invisible adjustment of the horizontal trim tab. "I know all that, Ed, and I've been thinking about it. Probably Colonel Williams knows too. But if I had to make the decision again, I'd call it the same way. How about you?"

"No argument."

"We're not on the ground yet, but we started this thing, we taxied it, we got it off the ground, and we've flown it a good distance. So we can land it. After that, maybe Father Ferrara will put in a good word for us."

Chang held out his left hand. "Dick, I'm with you all the way, you know that."

Sylvester took his hand and gripped it tightly. "Ed," he said, his throat tense—and left it at that.

The C-130 came in on the headsets. "Four niner hotel, you have another escort coming. Homestead is sending a T-33; as soon as he arrives, he will take over your control. Do you require any assistance from us?"

Sylvester answered. "Air Rescue three niner four, negative, but thanks for all the trouble in meeting us and guiding us this far."

"Four niner hotel, you're more than welcome. We'll stick around in case and if you need us, just holler. You may not see us, but we will be with you just the same."

"If you ever need the Civil Air Patrol, call on us," Chang cut in.

"Wilco, CAP four niner hotel, we need you all the time. Happy landings."

The C-130 moved forward rapidly, rose higher, and then drifted behind them.

"Here comes our new shepherd," Sylvester said and pointed. "At least a jet is headed our way."

"We seem to be generating most of the traffic around here," Chang commented. "Three jets and a Hercules."

The oncoming T-bird peeled off to the left, swung around and almost as if it had been rehearsed took up the same position that the C-130 had vacated only a short time before.

Ed remembered and turned the radio back to the emergency frequency. "Air Force T-bird, this is Connie four niner hotel," he said. It was a bad call, but he could not read the tail number of the Lockheed jet.

Apparently he was not heard, for in a moment the jet came in with its own call. "Hello, Connie four niner hotel, this is the T-33 alongside. Do you read me?"

"T-33 from four niner hotel, read you five by five."

"Good, switch to one two two decimal five. If no contact return to this frequency."

"This is where I came in," Sylvester said, over the intercom.

Ed retuned the set. "T-33, this is four niner hotel, how's this?"

"Just fine. Now let's drop the formalities; you don't have to give your number each time, O.K.?"

"Fine with us," Chang answered.

"Then let's get acquainted. Who is the aircraft commander?"

"Captain Richard Sylvester, Civil Air Patrol." Dick answered for himself. He put a little bite into his words without knowing why he did so. As soon as he had, he regretted it.

"What do your friends call you, Captain?"

"Dick."

"Fine, let's use that. Who is the other crew member?"

Sylvester nodded that Chang should answer that question. "I'm Ed Chang, lieutenant, CAP."

"Fine, Ed, glad to meet you. Gentlemen, I'm Sam Aschenbrenner, major, United States Air Force. That last name is a rough one, so just call me Sam."

"Fine, Sam," Chang said.

"Now, Dick, I'm also a Connie aircraft commander."

"Thank God for that!" Sylvester said. "Will you answer some questions for us?"

"That's why I'm here. Now let me check on some things. First, just the two of you make up the crew for this flight, is that right?"

"Yes, sir," Sylvester said. His throat was a little dry, but at least he had not forgotten how to address a superior officer. He thought that Ed Chang's quick use of the major's first name was a little too free, despite the major's invitation to do so.

"Secondly, I get the word that your elevator boost mechanism is out, is that correct?"

"Affirmative."

"Does the control yoke flop back and forth freely for a few degrees and then stop dead?"

"Yes, sir, exactly."

"Thank you. Now we're over Nassau and will have to change heading. Follow us."

The little jet, wheels and flaps down, swung to the left. It was an easy turn and Dick Sylvester had no trouble banking the Connie and lining it up again with the guide plane when he rolled it out. He felt particularly cool and professional as he did so. Having a Connie pilot available to consult had made a great change in his outlook.

"Good turn, who's flying?" the T-bird came through.

"I am, Sylvester," Dick answered.

"All right. Now somebody must have been at the flight

engineer's station when you took off. Who was it?"

"I did that, Ed Chang," the lieutenant answered.

"Are you both pilots?"

"Affirmative," Chang answered.

"Ed, I'd like you to return to the flight engineer's station now and fasten your seat belt. Dick, you'll have to do the flying alone. Is that O.K.?"

"Whatever you say."

"One more thing, before we firm this up, which of you has the most multi-engine experience?"

"Neither of us has any," Sylvester replied. "Before today, that is."

If Aschenbrenner had any reaction to that statement, he did not reveal it. "Then which of you has the most air time, and how much?" he asked.

"I've got a little over six hundred hours," Sylvester replied. "Ed has about half that, I believe."

"Are you both rated CAP pilots?"

"Yes, sir, affirmative."

"That's a big help. As long as you follow me exactly, and keep your wits about you, I see no real problem."

"I hope not, sir," Sylvester said.

"Now, if you don't mind, Dick, I'm going to usurp some of your authority as aircraft commander and take over the direction of your flight from out here. I know the Connie pretty well. With a major control system out you have an emergency situation and there isn't too much margin for error."

"You take over," Sylvester said, relieved. "We'll follow your instructions."

"Good. Now if at any time you lose communication with me, call immediately on one two one decimal five, the international emergency frequency. Somebody will hear you."

"We know about that."

"I'm glad to hear it. Now, is Ed at the flight engineer's station and if so, can he hear me?"

"I'm here and you're coming in just fine," Chang reported.

"Then we're all set up. Now, do you have the procedures handbook aboard?"

The lieutenant answered. "Yes, we have the ops manual. We've been studying it, believe me."

"Just the thing you should have done. Next, do you have a separate checklist on cards? Look on the backs of the crew seats."

"We have a checklist; it's in a little roller box at the co-pilot's station."

"In that case, forget it. Open the manual to the approach checklist. You shouldn't have any trouble finding it."

"I've got it here," Chang responded after a pause. "By now I knew where to look."

"All right, Ed, now listen carefully: I want you to read each item to me beginning at the top and don't skip a thing, no matter what. After each one I'll advise you what to do."

"Yes, sir, I'm ready."

"Stand by. Before we begin the checklist, Dick, I want you to follow us. We will be turning to a heading of one eight zero degrees."

"That's straight south," Sylvester said.

"I'm aware of that. I need time to complete the checklist with Ed and you. Also I'm going to give you two or three practice approaches here at altitude to give you the feel of the aircraft."

"How long will we be flying south, away from Miami?" Sylvester asked.

"I can't say. Suppose you leave that to me. Are you low on fuel?"

"No fuel problem, but we have some medical patients on board who urgently need attention. If you will tell us when to put the gear and flaps down, sir, and how much, I think we can get this thing down all right."

There was a short pause before there was an answer.

"No, Dick, you can't," Aschenbrenner said. "I think I'd better give it to both of you straight. Are you reading me?"

"Yes, sir."

"All right, we'll turn first. Follow us."

The T-33 rocked its wings for a moment and then turned southward over the Gulf Stream, away from the westerly heading toward Miami and Homestead. Reluctantly, but knowing that it was necessary, Dick lowered the left wing of the airliner and let the big plane swing around. He was anxious now to have the thing over with; the thought kept pressing him that the longer he and Ed were in flight in this big aircraft, the more the complications would pile up on them. His concern was augmented by the appearance of the western sky. The sun hung very low and if they flew around too much longer he would be stuck with a night landing. In the light plane business one didn't usually fly at night, not in single-engined aircraft at least. As a consequence he had had no night experience whatever. It seemed to him wise to mention this to the major.

He picked up the microphone. "I'm not checked out in night landings."

"I can't help that," Aschenbrenner came back. "Now get this, and understand me clearly. I don't believe that either of you realize the spot that you're in. I'll give you full credit for getting the bird off the ground and for flying it up this far.

But it's been by the grace of God. I'm not belittling your abilities, or your brains, but you've had an angel under each wing and Saint Peter holding up the tail."

"I didn't think it was that bad," Sylvester said, holding down the mounting anger in his voice.

Aschenbrenner ignored him. "Just because the professionals do it every day and make it look easy, don't get the idea that a Connie is easy to fly. Not without proper training, that is. But that's only a small part of it. Now you've got to land it. Take-offs are easy, you should know that.

"You've been exceptionally lucky that you didn't hit any bad weather, particularly with a full-blown hurricane on the rampage in the area," the major went on. "But all this is academic against the job you have to do to set that thing down."

Sylvester could keep still no longer. "I've landed planes a good many times, sir," he said.

"Of course you have. I assumed that. But landing a light aircraft and putting a Connie on the runway are two wholly different things."

"I planned on coming in a lot faster," Sylvester added, "and I know I will have to flare higher using the trim tab. I've been thinking it out carefully."

"Dick, I don't think you get the point," Aschenbrenner said patiently. "Landing a Connie is nothing like putting down a light plane. If you tried to put that plane you're flying now on the ground just as you said, using the technique you have learned, you'd kill yourself and every soul on board with you. A Connie can't glide for one thing the way the planes you have been flying do. It's a totally different thing you don't even begin to understand. Am I being too rough?"

"No, go ahead."

146

"All right. Now I am hoping to almighty God that I can rehearse you out here well enough that there will be a fighting chance to get you, all of your passengers, and your bird on the ground in something approaching a safe condition. If you keep your heads about you, perhaps we can do it together."

He waited, but there was no answer from the Super-Constellation.

"You see, Dick," he concluded, "with a major control system out even the best Connie pilot in the world would declare an immediate emergency and use every bit of his experience and skill to land safely. As yet you don't have that skill. I don't want to frighten you, but you need to understand clearly that if you make the least mistake when you get into the landing phase, disaster can overtake you so fast you'll never know what happened."

"It really is that bad?" Sylvester asked. He was hanging on to the control yoke harder now and his knuckles felt the strain of his mounting tension.

"Yes, it is. If you had tried to go straight in on your own, the chances are better than even you would have had about fifteen minutes left to live."

Chapter Twelve /

DORIS WONG SAT VERY STILL, LOOKING DOWN
at her hands, which were folded in her lap. Many different
thoughts were surging through her mind and she was making an almost desperate effort to sort them out.

The first was a sense of guilt. She had told all of these
people, most of whom were total strangers, that she was going to be Ed's bride—but she had yet to tell him. It was not
fair that he should have to come after so many others, when
it was his right to be the first. But of course the general had
asked her, and under the circumstances she had had little
choice but to tell the truth.

Next, she could not help wondering if what she had to offer
would be enough. She had little confidence in herself as a

physical being. When a man married he was entitled to a wife who could and would be everything to him. She had seen a picture of the first girl who had visited a Chicago beach in a topless bathing suit. She had been arrested, of course, this being America, but not before someone had taken the picture of a very lovely girl with beautifully formed breasts. Doris felt that when people talked about "curves" that was what was meant. Her own breasts were tiny, so much so that she had no real need to wear a brassière. She had once tried one which contained some subtle padding to give her more of a figure. Ed had taken her out the night that she had worn it. She thought he had not noticed, but then when he had kissed her good night he had whispered to her, "You don't need it, baby. I like you too much the way you really are."

Of course she had thrown it away before she went to bed.

She flexed her fingers to give her eyes something to look at. Then she thought about her slender hips and wondered if she were properly equipped for marriage. Of course many small women became mothers. Look at the population of China!

If Ed did not like her after they were married, then she would make it easy for him to find someone else. She nodded and looked up, then she glanced at her watch. It was eight minutes after the hour.

The general was looking at her. As she met his gaze, and read what was written there, she asked, "He will be all right, won't he?" Her voice was clear and quiet.

The general nodded, but only after a very brief pause. "I think so, Miss Wong. At the same time I know you understand that there are problems."

"But Ed is a wonderful pilot," she defended. "He hasn't

been flying too long, but everything he does he does right. He has a great gift."

"I'm most happy to hear that." The square-cut man in the fitted blue uniform answered her calmly. "But it isn't a question of his ability, or of his companion's. It's the fact that they aren't properly trained for what they are trying to do. It's a little like a talented beginner on the violin trying too soon to play a concerto with a symphony orchestra."

"I know that he is flying a much bigger plane than he has flown before, but is there *that* much difference?"

The general pursed his lips and leaned back to look at the ceiling for a moment. "Yes, Miss Wong, there is. You see, the difference isn't simply a matter of size. If that were all that is involved, it would be a relatively simple matter."

"Please tell me more about it," she asked.

"Are you sure you really want me to?"

"Yes."

"All right. First of all, then, instead of one simple engine he has to contend with four powerful, complicated ones." He looked at Colonel Williams. "What is the approximate horsepower of the plane Lieutenant Chang was flying when he departed your field?"

"About a hundred," the CAP commander answered.

"And the prop?"

"Wood, fixed pitch."

The general looked back at the girl. "The plane your future husband is flying weighs about seventy tons at a guess with the fuel and load he has on board. That's more than a hundred times the bulk weight of the L-6 or of probably anything else he has ever flown.

"But as I told you sheer size isn't the problem. Instead of one engine of a hundred horsepower he has four R3350-91 turbo-compound power plants, each one of which can deliver more than three thousand horsepower."

"A hundred and twenty times as much," Doris said.

"Exactly, but each of these engines has many systems and controls with which he and his co-pilot are probably totally unfamiliar. Then the propellers, instead of being simple fixed blades of wood, are highly-sophisticated mechanisms with de-icing equipment, variable pitch controls, and they can be reversed to drag instead of pull forward.

"Now in a simple plane like the L-6 there is no hydraulic system unless there is a very elementary one to work the brakes. I'm not sure on that point. But on the C-121, or the Super-Constellation, there is a very complex hydraulic system which controls the landing gear, the wing flaps, and the whole power boost system. It takes quite a while to learn to operate it properly even with mock-up boards and expert instruction.

"Then there are the electrical systems. In the L-6 there might be as much as two hundred feet of wiring, largely to work the navigation lights. In the Connie there are miles of circuits which control a hundred different things about the aircraft. There is a pressurization system, an anti-icing system, an air-conditioning system, a power boost system, a fire control system, all of which will be totally new and strange to him. Am I frightening you?"

"No, please go on."

"If you so desire. If this Connie is equipped as I suspect it is, if he pulls the wrong handle he can deploy a life raft in the wing and create a hellu—I beg your pardon, a very serious drag problem when the thing inflates automatically in the slipstream."

He looked a question mark at Toolie Sims, who nodded his head affirmatively.

"There is no need of dragging this out, Miss Wong. I

could go on for another ten minutes. Normally it takes at least three highly-skilled men to operate a Constellation flight. Your man and his partner are each handling a fifty percent overload, without knowing what they are doing at least ninety percent of the time and—" he paused and once more stared at the ceiling for another moment—"they are flying with one of the three basic flight control systems totally inoperative. Now that's the black of it. Would you like to have me paint you the other side of the picture?"

"No, sir," Doris answered, "I don't think that will be necessary. You see, sir, I know Ed—Lieutenant Chang."

The general tipped forward and planted his feet on the carpeting, the position which he unconsciously assumed when he had to administer a reprimand or deliver an important decision.

"Miss Wong," he said, "when you are married, will you do me the honor to invite me to be present at the ceremony?"

"Why, certainly." Doris was for the moment slightly off balance. "It would be a great honor for us if you were to come. But may I ask why?"

"Because," the general said firmly, "I specifically want to kiss the bride."

Despite the grimness of the warning they had been given, Ed Chang still felt that they were doing all right. So far they had been smart enough to leave alone all of the buttons, handles, and gadgets they had not actually needed, and they were almost in sight of the mainland. With five hours of instruction he felt that he would be capable of handling the whole flight engineer's station. Of course the five hours of instruction weren't available before their landing, but the T-bird alongside would supply the essential data.

"Ed, are you there?" the T-bird asked.

"Affirmative," he answered.

"Let's go ahead. What is the first item on your approach checklist?"

"Altimeter setting," Chang read off.

"You ought to know how to do that. Set both pilot's and engineer's altimeters to two niner decimal eight six. Now what do you read on yours, Ed?"

"Seventy-nine hundred feet."

"Dick?"

"Right on eight thousand," Sylvester answered.

"That's well within limits; don't worry about the difference. Next item."

"Seat belt and no smoking signs," Chang reported.

"They're over your head, Dick, to the right," Aschenbrenner directed. "Don't get the landing lights; they're up there too."

Sylvester allowed himself the luxury of feeling professional as he coolly looked up and flipped the two clearly-marked switches. "Signs on," he reported, recovering a little of his composure.

"Now, Dick, until we have completed the checklist, I want you to be sure and maintain at least one six zero knots airspeed, using your throttles for power. What rpm are you showing now?"

Still feeling more strongly in possession of himself, Dick replied, "We've held twenty-three hundred for the whole flight. We took a guess at the correct value. That seemed to go all right, so we used it."

"That setting will do for now, but don't exceed thirty-five inches of manifold pressure. Do you understand about that?"

Dick carefully inspected the panel before he answered. "I

have the gauges located. I'll try to watch them."

"Don't just try, Dick, this is very important. Keep your eye on the airspeed and manifold pressure. Look at them every few seconds."

"All right, sir."

"That's fine. To help you out, we will monitor your airspeed for you from here. You're in good shape and doing fine. Ed, what's the next item on your list?"

"Flight control auxiliary booster switches."

"Dick, you will have to handle this one. They are right next to the NO-SMOKING sign, *but be sure and leave the elevator boost off!* It's plainly marked."

Once more Dick reached up, not quite so certain this time. He pushed a switch and a light immediately showed. "I have thrown one switch," he reported. "A little yellow light came on. Is that O.K.?"

"Yes, but be sure that the elevator auxiliary booster is off."

Dick looked carefully once more. "Check, it's off—the one on the left."

"Fine, next item."

"Wing flaps," Chang reported.

"Hold them for now. What follows?"

"Manual spark."

"Leave that alone. Go on."

"Engine blowers."

"Leave them in low, repeat low. Ed, the handles should be in the middle position. They are right next to the field tank selectors. Do you see them?"

Chang grinned. "Right, I've already got 'em set into position."

"Next?"

"Mixtures."

"Yours, Ed. They're the red handles right next to the blowers. They should be full forward."

"That's where they are," Chang reported. "They've been that way all along."

"Real fine. What's next?"

"Fuel tank selectors."

"Ed, this is yours again. They're the four black handles to the right of the mixtures. Push all four all the way forward."

This time Ed did not report them in position; actually he had two of them forward, the other two back. He tried to remember why he had set them that way, but he could not recall. He debated whether he had better report the fact and decided to play it safe, just in case. He would be a fool to do anything else. "I just pushed the two in the middle all the way forward. Is that correct?"

"Yes, that puts you on your landing tanks. Now while you are at it, Ed, look on the upper panel in the center for a fuel gauge called the totalizer. It is the large one in the center, second row down. Do you see it?"

Chang made certain he had the right one. "Got it," he announced.

"What does it read?"

"Call it three hundred or a shade over."

"That means you have plenty of fuel left, thirty thousand pounds of it, so no sweat there. Also that added weight will make your elevator-boost-out landing easier. What's next?"

"Fuel pumps." At that moment Ed Chang realized that thirty thousand pounds of fuel was fifteen tons of it. That would be a helluva lot to spill if anything went wrong. And if a spark hit it . . . The voice from the T-bird cut him off from his thoughts.

"O.K., they're the little toggle switches right below your

fuel tank selectors, the last levers you moved. See them?"

"Right."

"Put them all in high. Next item."

Sylvester noted that he was drifting slightly off his heading; he tried to correct it as inconspicuously as possible. Aschenbrenner must have a lot of time in a Connie to know the whole thing the way he did from memory. A sudden thought hit Sylvester, and he acted on impulse.

"What would happen if I *did* throw the elevator boost switch?" he asked. "If the thing doesn't work anyway, what difference would it make?"

"You'd lose all your hydraulic fluid and wouldn't be able to get the gear down for one thing." Despite the air-to-air transmission, Dick Sylvester caught the sharp edge to the words, and his confidence ebbed a little. He hadn't thought of that possibility. He shook his head.

"Next, rpm," Chang said.

"All right for the present."

"Is there much more of that list?" Sylvester asked Ed, a little anxiously. The problems seemed endless.

"Quite a lot more. Several items anyway."

Sylvester looked out and over his right shoulder toward the setting sun. It was already gone. The red glow in the sky where it had been caused him to tighten up, and he pressed his teeth hard together.

"It's getting dark," he said over the air.

"I understand," Aschenbrenner answered. "Now we're going to get set for an approach, so set your prop controls, Dick, for twenty-four hundred turns."

Reaching over with his right hand Sylvester moved the stiff handles. The engines seemed to respond rather than the propeller blades; he had the feeling he had not done this too well. "I've got them set," he reported, "but it seems a lot noisier."

"That's O.K. You're probably a little out of sync. Don't let it bother you. Before you land, we're going to twenty-six hundred anyway."

Sylvester looked at Chang, who looked back. That couldn't be right, and they both knew it.

"*Faster* to land?" Sylvester asked.

"Yes, that's right. Now you can go to thirty-seven inches manifold if you need to, Dick. Use your throttles for air speed control."

Sylvester looked quickly at the manifold pressure gauges with the guilty knowledge that he had not been monitoring them as he should. He would have to do better than that.

"What does your manifold pressure read right now?" the major asked.

"Twenty-nine inches."

"Real fine, that's a good setting. What's next, Ed?"

"Brakes."

"Just look at the co-pilot's panel and make sure there are no red lights on. If you can see the hydraulic gauge on the right side, read me the pressure."

The man in the T-bird had the memory of a computer, Chang thought. "Sixteen hundred I make it."

"The one on the left should read the same."

"It does."

"We're on the rails. Next?"

"Tank five and crossfeeds." For the life of him he had no idea what that meant other than the obvious fact that it had something to do with the fuel supply.

"See the levers down by your left hand, Ed? Push them all the way toward the nose of the aircraft."

"All five of them?"

"Right, all five, all the way forward. Next."

"Pressurization."

"Did you do anything with the air-conditioning and pressurization panel?"

"No, we left it strictly alone. We decided before we took off not to touch anything we didn't actually have to."

"That was a smart decision. Now look on the panel in front of you, the one up above you, and the air-conditioning panel. Do you see any red lights on any of them?"

"I don't see a one," Ed answered. He sensed that a red light meant something wrong, and he was proud that there was not a single one to point at.

"Excellent, Ed. Now if you do see one, let me know right away as soon as it comes on, no matter what. That's very important, understand?"

"Yes, sir, I do."

"Now you are probably getting tired of this checklist, but the whole thing must be done and done correctly, you realize that, don't you?"

"Yes," Sylvester cut in, "but since we are this close, I want very much to get this thing on the ground. Our patients need attention."

This time the major answered quietly. "It is my job to get you down safely, Dick. You probably don't realize it, but all of these systems *must* be in the proper configuration or you could be in a lot more trouble than you are now. A Connie isn't a simple airplane, you know."

"I'm beginning to find that out."

"Well, hang on, you'll be all right. What's next, Ed?"

"Autopilot servo levers," Chang answered clearly.

"Dick, this is your item. Reach down by your right leg

where you will find three black levers and one red one close together. *Don't touch the red one,* but make sure the three black ones are all the way up. Got it?"

Sylvester looked down and found them without trouble. "The black handles are already up," he advised.

"De-icer boots," Chang read off.

"Yours again, Dick. Reach down to the floor with your left hand and find a three-way switch. Do you have it?"

Sylvester tried, but apparently it was not there. "No," he answered.

"Ed, you will have to fly for a minute or two while Dick finds this. It's pretty well hidden—some of the controls on the Connie are intentionally kept out of sight."

Chang slipped into the co-pilot's chair and nodded that he was ready to take over. "I've got it," he said.

"Fine, now, Dick, reach down under the side shelf and find that switch. It should read 'Off' and no green light should show. The light is down by the switch."

Dick bent himself almost double and felt with his hands on the floor until he located the control, then he straightened up and reported. "This is Sylvester. I found the switch; it was off and no green light showed."

"Then that's all right. Ed, what's your next item?"

Regretfully Chang relinquished the controls, which he had had barely a minute, and returned to the engineer's station. "Approach minimums and field elevation."

"Skip that for now; go on."

Ed took a deep breath and let it out slowly. "Landing weight, CG, and speeds."

"This one I'll take," Aschenbrenner said. "Your landing weight is within limits. Are all your passengers seated to the rear of the plane?"

Chang answered. "Yes, as far as possible. Some are in the cargo compartment."

"Then your CG is fine. Maintain one hundred forty knots minimum during approach. I'll monitor that for you from here. We'll come over the fence at one twenty-five and touch down about one ten. That won't be hard, because you have an eleven-thousand-foot runway and half of that should do it. Anything else on your list?"

"No, that's it," Chang reported.

"Then we're ready for some practice approaches. Before we start, however, I suggest that you check the cabin and make sure that all the passengers are strapped in and ready for the landing."

"I'll call you when that's done," Chang said and took off his headset. He released his belt, glanced out at the darkening sky, and wondered about turning on lights. If he needed to, the major would tell him how. He opened the door to the cargo hold and stepped inside.

It was darker and somewhat cold. The dozen men in the hold were no longer interested in their flight; they sat silently most of them with their eyes closed, waiting.

Chang opened the remaining door to the main passenger cabin and stepped through. Father Ferrara was still on his feet; apparently he had never sat down. The lieutenant glanced up and saw that the two caution signs were both on. Next he looked quickly at Armando, afraid of what he would see. The young man appeared to be sleeping; his eyes were closed and his head was tilted to the side. The little girl apparently still slept too, with her mouth open wide, as she seemed to be trying to draw additional air into her small body.

The rest of the passengers were quiet. Many seemed to be

sleeping; one tiny baby was nursing at its mother's breast.

"When I saw the signs come on I pointed them out to everyone," the priest reported. "All are now fastened in; we await our first sight of your great country. Will it be long now?"

"We are almost there," Chang answered, keeping his voice low. "Do not be surprised if we put the wheels down and lift them back up again. Everything must be tested before we land, to be sure that it is all right." That was close enough to the truth to pass, and it might help.

"We have the greatest confidence in you, for have you not already brought us this far? You have truly led us beside the still waters. But I hope it will not be too long."

"Where is your seat, Father?" Chang asked.

"There is not one left, but it is no matter. I shall stand strongly in the aisle and hold hard to the seats. It will be all right; do not think further of me."

Silently Chang made his way down the aisle, checking each row of seats. He could do nothing about the several children in arms, but all of the adults and those who had seats to themselves were properly fastened in. He smiled and nodded at the tall priest and then closed the passenger cabin door softly behind him.

Back on the flight deck he put on his headset, adjusted the mike and pressed the button. "Cabin is secured," he reported. "Everyone is quiet for the moment."

Out of the gathering darkness the reassuring voice came back. "That couldn't be better. All right, Dick, let's do a gradual one eight turn to the right and roll out on a heading of magnetic north. I'll report we're on our way in."

Carefully Sylvester turned the yoke wheel toward the right. Outside the vast wing on his left lifted obediently upward and the massive airliner began to turn toward the last glow of the setting sun. As the nose of the aircraft swung slowly past the western sky there was little left of the daylight which a short while before had filled the sky. Sylvester knew that darkness would come rapidly and then he would no longer be able to see whether there was water or ground below. The horizon would disappear and his world would become the instrument panel before him.

If all went well he would find two long rows of lights in the blackness, lights which would mark the edges of the Homestead air base runway. Then it would be time for him to execute his first night landing, and without the familiar reference to the ground on which he had always depended in the planes he had previously flown. But others could do it, so he would do it too.

There was no choice; he *had* to. Unless he wanted to admit defeat and ask Ed Chang, with half his own experience, to attempt it.

He took a careful fresh grip on the control yoke, laid his right hand across the trim tab wheel, and resolved that he *would* do it, that somehow he would get this great, complex, badly-crippled, multi-ton aircraft safely on the ground.

His brow broke out in a sweat.

Chapter Thirteen /

"DICK, ARE YOU THERE?" CAME THROUGH the headset.

He pressed the microphone trigger on the control yoke. "I'm here."

"Since you're both doing so well, look on the overhead panel where the no-smoking and seat-belt sign switches are. Right underneath there should be a radio called 'VHF Nav,' do you see it?"

"Yes, it's there."

"Good. Turn the switch on and set in one one seven decimal one."

He turned the dial.

The voice came in again. "That's called an omni set, gentlemen, and will show you at all times a relative bearing to Biscayne Bay. Dick, on your instrument panel do you see a radio compass with a needle on it?"

"Where is it located?" Sylvester asked.

"It should be at the five o'clock position from your attitude indicator."

"Yes, O.K., I've got it."

"What bearing is the needle indicating now?"

"Three two zero degrees."

"Fine, I read three one eight on mine. If for any reason we get separated, home on that needle and it will take you right over Homestead Air Force Base."

Chang was silent, sitting at the engineer's station. Sylvester realized how hard it must be for him to do that, just to sit there when he must desperately want to be up front flying. He might have to stay there while he, Sylvester, made the landing. That would be the hardest thing of all.

Again the voice of Major Sam Aschenbrenner came out of the sky. "Dick, it's getting pretty dark, so you will want to get set up for a night landing. You aren't going to let this throw you, are you?"

"No sir, I'm not."

Ed Chang pressed his own mike button. "Don't worry about him, Sam," he said. "He's a good boy. You tell him, he'll do it."

"Right. I believe that. All right, Dick, it's time to turn on the inside lights; yours are on the left side, right by your arm, and are self-explanatory. The switches are all labeled. Ed, yours are overhead and are clearly marked also. Advise me when you have them turned on. Don't worry about the exterior lights for a moment, but check by the no smoking lights and find the position of the landing light switches."

"I have them located," Sylvester answered. He looked down to the left and had no difficulty in finding and turning on the interior lights.

"I saw them come on. Ed, up at the co-pilot's seat, by the hydraulic gauges I told you about find the switch marked *wing master lights.*"

In a moment Chang came back crisply. "Got it."

"Turn it on, use the position marked *steady and bright,* then return to the flight engineer's station. You're doing two jobs right now, whether you know it or not."

"No sweat," Chang answered.

Aschenbrenner's voice continued in a steady tone. "Dick, on the left-hand panel, where the interior lights are, turn on the wing top, tail light, and leading edge light. I want this last one so we can keep track of you more easily as it gets darker. Good, I just saw them come on."

Chang once more fastened his seat belt at the engineer's station and glanced through the windshield. Then he looked over his shoulder at the western sky and saw the bright pinpoint of light that was the planet Venus. Quite a long day they were having in the air. A lot of time to write in their log books.

Aschenbrenner was with them again. "We're all set for some practice approaches. Now in a Connie when you drop flaps, you balloon and the air speed falls off rapidly, so be ready for this."

"What do I do?" Sylvester asked.

"Just anticipate adding more power when the flaps reach sixty percent and the air speed drops off. Understand?"

"I think so."

"To the right of the throttles is the flap handle. Do you see it?"

Sylvester nodded and then realized that that wouldn't do. "I've got it," he reported.

"Now note where the sixty percent mark is on the pedestal. Pull the flap handle back to the first detent, which is sixty percent. Watch for a balloon, do you feel it?"

In response to the command Sylvester took hold of the handle and moved it very carefully down to the moment when he felt the slight detent. Underneath him the great bird abruptly began to rise. He let go of the flap handle and grabbed for the horizontal trim wheel. The upward motion continued, the altimeter needle reacted and the rate of climb swung sharply upward.

"Yes!" he answered.

"Add power to maintain a hundred and sixty knots," Aschenbrenner warned sharply. "It takes a little getting used to, flying with the flaps down."

Sylvester did not answer. Suddenly the aircraft he had been flying had changed into something else entirely, with a mind of its own, which responded in a totally new manner.

"Need help?" Chang asked.

"I'll hack it," Sylvester said, but his voice was tight with concentration.

Once more words came out of the night. "Practice elevator trim a little in this attitude, but don't take too long. When you're ready to drop the gear, let me know. You're doing real fine, but let's come back down to eight thousand, where we were."

Gear down would add a new flying characteristic and Sylvester had his hands more than full with the one he had now. "I don't know if I can set this thing down," he heard himself saying. "I was sure I could, but now . . ."

The voice came back sharp and clear. "Nonsense, of course

you can! I'm just setting you up to make a real good one, a grease job, understand?"

Sylvester tried to pull himself together. "All right, I'll do my best. I guess I'm ready for the gear."

"That's the stuff. Pull back your power a little and slow down to one fifty. When I tell you, push the gear handle down."

"What will happen?" Sylvester asked.

"It'll be all right, just keep on that elevator trim and be ready to add power, because the gear adds a lot of drag in a Connie. Ed, you better handle the power."

"I will," Chang answered quickly.

"O.K., gear down."

Sylvester held his teeth hard together and pulled downward on the wheel-shaped handle. It refused to move.

"I can't, it won't work!" he almost shouted.

"My fault." Aschenbrenner came back almost on top of his words. "I forgot to tell you to pull back on the handle and then down. You'll have to trim back on the elevator while Ed adds some more power."

Sylvester, jaw clenched, pulled out the handle and pushed it firmly down. There were immediate mechanical noises from under the floor of the cockpit, the indicator showed striped shields in the three windows, and then three black and white discs appeared. He felt the drag of the extended gear and, as Aschenbrenner had said, he had to roll the stabilizer back to re-establish the trim. He heard the power of the engines gain as Ed Chang advanced the set of throttles at the engineer's station. Good for Ed; he always came through!

"Now that wasn't so bad, was it?" Aschenbrenner asked.

Sylvester licked his dry lips. "No, but I'm glad now we're

practicing first. It would have thrown me if I had tried to do that for the first time close to the ground."

"Then we're making progress. Did the little red lights on the console go out?"

"I don't see any red lights."

"Look under number three and four tachometer and be sure the gear is down and locked. You should see three wheels in the windows."

"They're there."

"All right. Ed, do you see the cylinder head temperature gauges right in front of you?"

"They're reading two hundred degrees," Chang answered.

"That's all right. Now note the cowl flap switches on your left. If the head temperatures get above two hundred, open the flaps. If they get below one eighty, close them. You will have to watch this and do it, engine by engine."

Aschenbrenner continued, putting a little more urgency into his voice. "Now pull the power back to twenty-two inches and let the air speed fall off to a hundred and twenty knots. This is the over-the-fence speed. Get the feel of it, but don't let it fall any lower."

"Wilco." A moment later Sylvester added, "I'm losing altitude!"

"You should. Now add power to thirty-five inches and raise the gear."

Chang pushed the throttles forward, then in one motion loosened his seat belt, raised himself up, and reaching out his arm pushed the gear lever up so that Sylvester would not have to let go of the flight controls.

"Check the indicator to be sure the gear is up. Also note the trim change and how the air speed is increasing. When you feel comfortable, raise the flaps and add power to indicate a hundred and eighty knots."

Chang watched and waited until he saw that Sylvester had the big bird fully under control, then he eased up the flaps and fed in additional power until the air speed was almost exactly on the 180 mark. He felt better because he was doing something, and, like Sylvester, learning a bit more about the aircraft they had undertaken to fly.

Aschenbrenner spoke to them again. "We have just been cleared to descend to four thousand. Drop your flaps to sixty degrees and let her sink. You know how now, so this should be easy."

Sylvester nodded that he would do this himself. He reached over and with somewhat more confidence moved the flap handle down. He did not have his hand off the lever before an ear-splitting noise blasted the relative quiet of the cockpit. In spite of himself Sylvester gripped the wheel hard as though something should be done with it to stop the sudden violence to his ears.

Ed Chang, who did not have to fly, looked quickly about him to see if a window had blown open again. But this was a different kind of noise, something from within the cockpit itself. Then, remembering what he had read, he guessed at the cause. He raised the flap handle and shortly the noise cut off as sharply as it had come.

"When we put the flaps down, we got a very loud noise," Chang said into his microphone. He was proud of the understatement.

"Gear warning," Aschenbrenner replied. "You probably pushed the flap handle down to eighty percent instead of sixty. Try it again." It sounded to Sylvester as though the major's tone was a little shorter, and had been for the last two or three transmissions. The strain on the major must be tremendous. Sylvester reached over and lowered the flap handle once more, being careful to feel the detent. There was no answering blast of sound, so this time he had done it right. He held the aircraft steady and watched the altimeter unwind.

"Are you all trimmed up?" Aschenbrenner asked.

"Yes, sir," Sylvester answered. "These dry runs are a great help. I'm beginning to get the feel. One more and I think I will be on top of this thing."

"I'm glad you feel better," Aschenbrenner answered. "But there won't be any more dry runs, Dick. This is it. We are running low on fuel out here and just about have enough left to see you safely in."

Sylvester swallowed hard. Now he knew that he had had his swings at batting practice and it was for keeps from here on in. He looked over at Ed Chang for a sign of reassurance, and got it.

"Let's have a little more power," Aschenbrenner directed. "Keep on descending. We have just been cleared all the way. You are number one to land."

Sylvester remembered the omni radio he had turned on; he looked at the needle and saw that the relative bearing was almost dead ahead, 360 degrees. "When did we turn?" he asked.

"While you were trying out the flaps and gear you got a little off your heading. Since it was in the right direction, I just let you come around. Now are you reading me clearly?"

"Yes, sir."

"All right, we are now making our approach to the field. You will land on runway 5, conditions are VFR, so you should have no trouble at all picking it up. Are you familiar with the appearance of lighted runways at night?"

"I've seen a few."

"Then you know what to look for. Now don't get up a sweat. You have over eleven thousand feet on which to land and what's more it's three hundred feet wide. You have plenty of room, understand?"

Sylvester tried to let the thought that he had a long, wide runway to land on soak in. He focused on that thought to bring his mind into line, and to push back the concern which was once more beginning to build steadily within him. He had known when he proposed to take off that he would have to land, but he had rationalized that it would all work out automatically. Now he had made his take-off and had largely done his flying. The landing was before him; it would not go away and it would not be denied.

He glanced at the altimeter; it shook him to read twenty-eight hundred feet. Five thousand feet of altitude had slipped away with his present flaps-down condition and it had taken so little time! That was the trouble with landing: so many things happened at once, and so fast. He wished to heaven that Ed could be up here with him, to lend him moral support if nothing else. He was alone, desperately alone, and he felt the suppressed concern taking hold of him now and filling him up as though it were a liquid and he was an empty container into which it was being poured.

The voice from the T-bird came in again to remind him of what he must do. "Dick, you need more power. Come up to twenty-four inches."

"I'll do it," Chang said quickly. The sharpness in his voice told Sylvester that Chang had read him and understood—that he knew the strains which were mounting within him.

The engines responded to the added ration of fuel and picked up the tempo of their controlled roar.

"Ed, you're needed up front now; take the co-pilot position."

Sylvester was almost pathetically grateful for that; now Ed was coming to join him. He took his eyes off the instruments to watch his partner seat himself and snap the lap belt lock shut. Somehow it seemed that Ed would double his own flying resources, add his experience on top of what he, Sylvester, could already command. Perhaps Aschenbrenner had thought along these lines too.

Ed spoke into his microphone. "Chang. I'm in co-pilot's position. We have twenty-four inches of manifold."

"Good boy. Let's have the before-landing checklist."

Chang reached up to the little scroll box, found the light switch, and illuminated the items to be read off. "Rpm," he reported.

"Set the lever next to the throttles to twenty-six hundred turns."

Chang reached out and complied with what seemed to Sylvester to be total confidence. His voice conveyed the same thing when he spoke. "Right. Twenty-six hundred set. Next item is landing gear. Shall I put it down now?"

"Yes. Dick, don't descend below fifteen hundred until I tell you. I have the glide slope indicator on over here. Intercept altitude is one five hundred for the Homestead ILS."

Sylvester looked again quickly at the altimeter; it read seventeen hundred feet. He knew what ILS was, but he had nothing set up. His composure deserted him and he spoke without thinking. "I don't have any ILS!"

"Yes you do, but don't worry about it—this will be a contact landing. We'll guide you in. Now level off here."

Sylvester shook his head to clear his brain and tried to pull back on the yoke. It reached the apparent stop and would go no farther. Then he remembered once again that he could not control the elevator, only the trim tab. He reached for the tab wheel and rolled it back a few degrees. The realization hit him that now, at the worst of all possible times, the airplane was flying him instead of his flying the airplane. He must, *must* do better!

Chang pulled out the gear lever and pushed it down. Once more thumping, pounding sounds came from under the floor; the panel indicator showed its barber poles and then cleared up. Three wheels appeared in the windows.

"Gear down," Chang reported as Sylvester once more rolled the trim tab back to compensate for the added drag.

"Does it show down and locked on the panel?"

"Yes, sir," Chang answered. Sylvester thought there was almost a happy note in his voice. Who did he think he was anyway, Scott Crossfield? "Indicator checks down; the light is out. Next item is landing lights."

"Extend them, Ed. The switches are up above near the no-smoking sign. Push them forward to the marked position. I'll tell you when to turn them on. That completes the checklist, right?"

"Right!"

"Now turn on your panel lights, on the right-hand panel."

"Already on." Chang's confidence seemed unbounded.

"You're all set up, couldn't be better. Now look ahead, gentlemen, and you can see the field."

Sylvester lifted his head and looked. He did not see it at first, then apparently far ahead there was a pathetically thin double row of lights which marked the two sides of the runway.

"I see the field," Sylvester said with a new strained tone in his voice. "I'll approach just as you tell me to. Then I'll attempt to land. If for any reason I botch the job, then I'll go around and try it again."

Aschenbrenner came back with authority in his voice. "No, Dick, that won't do. For one thing we don't have enough fuel to stick with you on a go-around. And in a Connie it's complicated and involves special problems of its own. You're lined up now as well as you ever will be. You will land on this first pass unless I tell you otherwise, and that's an order!"

When the T-bird called that it was twelve minutes out, Major Ben Griffin shifted into high blower as he was already prepared to do. He gave the *go* signal to position all equipment and facilities for a crash landing. At once the machinery which he had set up went into action.

On the ramp the compact, turbine-powered HH-43B rescue helicopter fired up and in seconds was airborne, hovering a few feet off the ground. It moved over to the fire suppression kit and hung in the air directly over it while a ground crewman ignored the downward blast of its twin rotors to hook the thousand-pound crash unit into position. When it had been secured the powerful little chopper hoisted it up and departed for its holding position near the end of the runway. Inside the rear cabin two highly-experienced rescuemen donned asbestos suits which would allow them, with a foaming hose in their hands, to walk directly into an aircraft fire and help those trapped on board to safety.

From their flight line garages the fire and crash trucks rolled massively out, their powerful engines making the night air throb. With red rotation beacons going they moved into position on the taxiways, the nozzles of their chemical hoses pointed at the landing runway in the direction from which the plane was to come. Two blue Air Force buses rolled up toward the end of the field to pick up the passengers, assuming that everything went well. Instructions had already been passed to the T-bird that the Connie was not to taxi after landing; it was to stop wherever it was and stay there. All other incoming traffic had been diverted for the emergency and the runway would be closed as soon as the Connie touched down.

In a staff car equipped with a command set Major Griffin directed the operation. He called the fire-fighting helicopter and moved it back farther from the runway. "Remember, these are unqualified amateurs flying," he warned. "Major Aschenbrenner reports they have never made a night landing. Keep back out of their way; they may miss the runway. Also your lights may confuse them."

For the same reason he backed the fire trucks almost to the ramp area. "If they can't control the aircraft on the ground, they may come off on the grass. If they hit one of you, then we've really got it. Give them all the room you possibly can."

Like the members of some huge mechanical ballet the fire and crash trucks moved backward together and kept their engines running so they could dash forward again as soon as the plane was safely opposite or past each of their positions.

Two ambulances swung out onto the ramp and took positions two-thirds of the way up the length opposite the runway.

"Who's the medical officer with you?" Griffin asked.

"Captain Gordon and Captain O'Keefe," one of the ambulances reported. Major Griffin wiped an arm across his brow and reflected that two doctors were better then one—especially if there might be several dozen patients all at once. Say eighty to be exact.

A shape showed up at the window of his command car; he looked up into the face of Major Solomon Lipschutz, the duty chaplain.

"Where do you want us?" the chaplain asked. "I have Captain Alvarez with me. Chaplain Alvarez speaks Spanish, and if there are casualties he can administer the last rites, should that be necessary."

"I'd say close to the ambulances would be the best spot," Griffin answered. "You might ride them if there is room."

The chaplain disappeared with no further words. He knew that as operations officer Ben had his hands full, with no time for extraneous conversation.

"Ten minutes out," the tower cut in and reported. "Radar has them approaching the glide path right on fifteen hundred."

"Good old Sam," Griffin said. It was a thankful prayer for the man in the T-bird, who was, indeed, one of the best.

A staff car bearing a starred plate in front rolled up beside him with three more in tow. General Ayms got out and leaned on the windowsill. "Where are we?" he asked.

"All emergency and rescue equipment is in position, sir," Griffin answered tersely. "The plane is about nine and a half minutes out. GCA reports them at fifteen hundred, right on the inbound track."

"Have they got the gear down?" the general asked.

Major Griffin picked up the microphone and spoke to the tower: in seconds he had the answer. "Major Aschenbrenner reports gear and flaps down. They are right on the rails, so the first pass should do it."

"Good, my heart is getting too old for this sort of thing."
He straightened up, looked about him in one sweeping
glance and then asked, "Chaplain?"

"Two—riding the ambulances."

"The HH-43B is orbiting with the FSK?"

"Yes, sir, back a little to give them more room."

"Medical officers?"

"O'Keefe and Gordon, both surgeons, in the ambulances."

The tower cut in on the radio. "Eight minutes. Still on
track."

"Colonel Aschenbrenner is with them?"

Griffin invisibly raised an eyebrow. "Colonel, sir?"

"Yes, that's not official yet, but it's gone through. Right
now I'd say he's earning it."

Ben Griffin knew the general well. "You're damn right he
is," he answered. "If he pulls this off you can pin a star on
him."

"Someday they probably will," the general answered, and
turned away. The staff cars behind his own had unloaded
their passengers; they stood in a little group all facing the
southwest end of the runway, waiting for something each
one of them feared to see.

"Come on, Connie," Bob Galloway said softly to himself.
"Come on, girl. You can make it. Just keep your nosewheel
up and don't let those two guys scare you." He didn't care
who heard. Airplanes were things with which he felt he
could communicate, and the few miles that separated them
would not hamper his Super-Constellation's power of understanding. He loved her, every rivet of her, and now she was
coming home to him.

Herb Stallings stared almost fiercely into the night as
though by doing so he could transmit some of his own skill

177

and understanding of Connie and her ways to the two amateurs who were trying to fly her. She was red-lined, but they
had got her this far, which made her one hell of a smart bird.
He didn't think about anything else; he just stood and
watched.

Scotty Zimmerman scanned the sky silently, saying nothing. Wilson stood beside him, and Sam Eastman, Zimmerman's co-pilot. Four police cars came onto the ramp, separated, and took up positions where they could see everything that was going on. Three more unmarked cars, un-
doubtedly authorized, also rolled onto the ramp and turned
toward the upper end of the runway.

Doris Wong, waiting and watching, fought desperately to
contain herself. She saw the general was also standing by
himself, and because he had been very kind to her she took
the few steps to be by his side.

"I'm frightened," she said.

"We all are," the general answered honestly, "but I have a
feeling they'll make it all right."

"Is Ed flying?" Doris asked.

"Yes, he is," the general answered instantly. "And he has
her right on the approach path, gear and flaps down, and all
set for a good landing. I couldn't do it any better myself."

Major Griffin opened the door of his staff car. "Five
minutes," he reported. "Dead on the approach path."

Doris moved a few inches closer to the general, her eyes
fixed immovably on the sky. The general raised his hand and
laid it on her shoulder, offering to share his strength with her.
She lifted her small hand and placed it on top of his.

Then, together, they saw far out two horizontal spots of
brightness come alive, the landing lights of the incoming
aircraft.

Chapter Fourteen /

"HOW ARE YOU FEELING?" SYLVESTER ASKED.

"Fine," Chang answered. "I like to fly, don't you?"

The reply was too confident. Sylvester guessed Chang was just trying to take things lightly.

Sylvester kept his eyes focused on the still-distant runway. He waited until he judged that he was almost lined up with it, then he dropped the right wing and let the plane slowly come around. Runway five meant that it was laid out on a heading of fifty degrees magnetic, which made it relatively easy to roll out on the right point.

"Nice turn," Aschenbrenner said from somewhere out in the blackness. "I was just going to tell you to do it."

It was good to hear that steadying voice again. "At least

we don't have a lot of traffic," Sylvester commented.

"No, you don't, because about thirty other planes have been diverted out of our way. A Jet Clipper just went the long way around to give you room; the pilot said to wish you good luck."

That didn't make Sylvester feel any better. It reminded him sharply once more that he had no business in the cockpit of a Super-Constellation.

Chang spoke. "Now, Dick, set her down nice and easy, and make the CAP look good."

Sylvester realized that he had forgotten all about the uniform he was wearing, and the twin silver bars which showed his rank. He passed his tongue over his dry lips.

Major Aschenbrenner cut his thoughts short. "All right, we're intersecting the glide path. Drop your flaps to eighty percent. The horn won't blow this time, because the gear is down."

Ed Chang reached with his left hand and lowered the flaps the additional twenty percent. Sylvester kept a cautious hand on the trim tab wheel and turned it a few degrees to re-establish the balance.

"Flaps eighty percent," Chang reported.

"Good," Aschenbrenner approved. "Now pull back on the power until you have established an approach speed of one hundred forty knots. Forget the manifold pressure. Don't pull back too much; take it real easy."

Sylvester unconsciously leaned forward, trying to watch the air speed indicator, the attitude indicator, and the runway well ahead all at the same time. He found it difficult.

"Don't worry about the power; I'll handle that," Chang said. "You just fly."

"You're a little below the glide path," Aschenbrenner

warned abruptly. "And trim her back a bit; you're doing one forty-five."

Sylvester made the correction, guessing at the proper amount.

Aschenbrenner came in again. "Now listen carefully, Dick, and remember what I say. Since you can't flare for your landing in the usual way with your elevator out, you're going to have to do it the hard way—with the trim tab."

"Yes, sir," Sylvester answered.

"To make it easier, I'm going to bring you in a little low and flat. Our over-the-fence target speed will be one twenty, got that?"

"One twenty, right."

"Now, just a little *before* the time you would usually begin your flare I want you to start feeling back on the trim tab control, not too much, a little does it. If you go too far, you could stall out in a hurry and with no elevator control you would have no chance to recover."

"You mean we would crash."

"Yes. Now, when the time comes, I won't be able to tell you exactly what to do because things will be happening too fast. It's going to be up to your judgment. Remember that you are flying a tricycle-gear airplane. Have you ever landed one before?"

"No."

"Come in normally, but don't try to get the tail down as you do in your light planes. Just hold the nosewheel off until the main gear is on. Then let the nose come down and feed in the brakes."

"I've got that," Sylvester said. He forced himself to speak calmly, praying that he would remember it all at the critical time.

"One more thing—as soon as your nosewheel is on, don't forget to steer it. Do you know how?"

"Yes, we practiced at take-off."

"Good. I'll try to help you all I can, but beginning from here on you are going to have to be pretty much on your own."

"Don't go away," Sylvester said. His throat tightened at the words and a sense of alarm touched him.

"I'll be close by, don't worry. I can't stay here on your wingtip without interfering with several things on the field. But I'll be watching every second."

"Dick, I have an idea," Chang said through the intercom.

"Make it fast, the field is getting closer," Sylvester answered. His voice was tight.

"Suppose you handle the ailerons, the rudder, the nose-wheel steering, and the brakes. I'll be responsible for the power and the horizontal trim tab."

Sylvester thought about it for two or three seconds. "You mean you'll make the flare?"

"If you think it's a good idea. That way you'll be able to fly with both hands. Otherwise with one hand on the tab control and the other on the yoke, you couldn't steer the nosewheel without making a double shift right after we hit."

Sylvester saw the sense of that. It would divide the responsibility right down the middle, but in this case it might be better that way. He suddenly didn't want to have to do it all himself.

"Let's do it," he said quickly. "But give me what I ask for fast if I need it."

"Of course. You're flying."

Sylvester lifted his hand from the trim tab and took a firm

hold of the main control yoke. Suddenly he did not have to worry about airspeed, and could concentrate on the runway up ahead. He had a co-pilot, and that was what co-pilots were for.

"Landing lights," Aschenbrenner ordered.

Grateful that he had a hand free, Sylvester reached up and turned them on. At once two sharply-defined funnels of light reached out in the sky, and into the blackness ahead.

"Good. You're holding your speed just fine. Who's flying?"

"We both are," Sylvester answered truthfully. "I'm taking the responsibility."

Whatever Aschenbrenner thought of that, he held his peace. For a few seconds it was dead quiet in the cockpit except for the sound of the four great engines, which now thundered in subdued voices.

"We are four minutes out," Aschenbrenner said. "Any questions?"

"No, sir," Sylvester answered. "But if we should abort, please tell us."

"You won't abort. Put that thought out of your mind. A little more to the right, Dick, you're fifty feet to the left of the glide path."

Sylvester lifted the left wing and let the aircraft slip over.

"Is that the way the CAP flies?" Aschenbrenner asked.

Sylvester felt very guilty. "No, sir, I know better. Where are you? I can't see you."

"Right above you. Down just a little now, we'll start dropping below the glide path so your flare will be easier and less critical."

"Right," Chang answered, "I'm holding twenty-three inches."

"Manifold twenty-three is good. Keep on coming, just as

you are." Aschenbrenner's voice was smooth and calm now.

The seconds ticked off on the panel clock; the altimeter showed eleven hundred feet.

"Three minutes," Aschenbrenner said.

Sylvester discovered that he was slightly to the left of the twin row of approaching lights; this time he carefully co-ordinated a slight turn and put the big plane back on the path. The nose sank perceptibly as Chang moved the elevator tab to maintain the airspeed. Sylvester glanced at the dial; it showed one thirty-eight. Ed was right on the ball.

"You're doing fine," Aschenbrenner came in evenly. "Any red lights showing?"

"Negative," Chang answered. "But I can't check the cylinder head temperatures from here."

"Never mind, you're all right. Just keep on as you are."

Sylvester felt a cold chill beginning to envelop him. It was a sensation which he had not experienced before. It seemed to him that some gigantic brake had been applied to his body, as though he could not make any motion without great effort and then with agonizing slowness.

He looked ahead at the runway. It appeared to have grown very slightly in length. From farther out it had looked chunky; now it was a little less so although it did not seem to be anything like two miles long. Nevertheless it was, he told himself, and that was what counted.

He looked at the gauges and read them quickly. Speed right on one forty, God bless Ed! Rate of descent: four hundred feet per minute. Altitude: eight hundred and dropping.

"Two minutes," the voice of Aschenbrenner said to him. "Surface wind is six knots, so forget it. Field elevation is only seven, repeat seven, feet, so consider it sea level. Altimeter two niner decimal eight zero."

Sylvester leaned forward to reset his altimeter to the new pressure; as he reached out Ed did the same.

"Ninety seconds."

Sylvester reached his hand out and confirmed the position of the nose steering wheel. It was right there at his left knee, with a blank radar scope tucked in behind it. With his toes he felt of the brakes at the top of the rudder pedals—those he knew how to use; they were just like the ones on Betsy. Once on the ground he would bear down on them and get the bird stopped as soon as he reasonably could. Never waste runway, he remembered the rule.

It was a marvel to Sylvester how smoothly the big aircraft slid down the glide path and he silently thanked God there were no clouds in the way. If he had had to make this approach with low cumulus or heavy nimbus clouds hiding the runway until the last minute, it would have been a different story.

"One minute," Aschenbrenner said very clearly. "Just a little more power now, Ed. Don't overdo it."

As Chang fed in a small amount of additional fuel Sylvester wondered abruptly how Aschenbrenner knew who was handling the engines. He had no time to speculate on it; the runway was now two miles ahead and it seemed to him that they were much too low. Which was why Aschenbrenner had called for more power, of course—the guardian angel was still there.

He looked at the airspeed—142.

All right, now the landing. He reminded himself that it would be higher and faster than in Betsy, but there was a longer, wider runway than he had ever used before, and it would be beautifully paved. He rehearsed quickly in his mind: in a tricycle-gear aircraft keep the nosewheel up until the main gear is firmly and finally on, then let it come down —and steer. After that, hit those brakes—there would be a lot of weight to stop.

He watched the runway and then, quite suddenly, it seemed to be coming closer at a much faster rate. Immediately he told himself that as he got nearer to the ground the apparent speed would increase. It was the same in a light aircraft although the speed itself was not nearly so great. His mind for a moment insisted on taking its own way: mass times velocity squared. He had a hundred times the mass he was used to, at least twice the velocity—more than four hundred times the total force . . .

Stop it!

Panic swept up like a sheet of flame; it seemed to envelop him, to blur his vision, to rob him of every power he possessed. Then he heard Chang speak.

"Here we go," Ed said, and for the first time his voice betrayed him.

Sylvester's panic receded as the twin cones of light from the wings reached the edge of the pavement and he could see the wide white stripes painted on the end. Above them, rushing to meet him, was the big 5 which identified the runway.

"Flare!" he yelled.

Suddenly everything was speed. The runway rushed up, the huge 5 seemed about to slap him in the face. Frantically he grabbed for the trim tab, but Ed was already rolling it back. He heard the roar of the engines slacken, but the power did not seem to come off. The red lights at the end of the runway swept underneath, the white stripes were swallowed up and gone, then the nose of the Constellation began to rise.

His muscles locked as he saw he was headed toward the side of the runway. He shoved the rudder hard and felt the plane begin to skid, then the nose came around and he was straight again, but a little to the side. He gulped in air and held his breath at that instant, not knowing what he was doing.

The runway continued to rush backward underneath, precious distance that was gone forever. He was desperate to chop the power and make the aircraft slow down, but Chang had his hands on the throttles. He felt the plane begin to sink and then with a hard impact the left main gear hit the ground.

Sylvester sensed it as the beginning of the crash; his right wing must be too high! He twisted the yoke to bring it down, but before the control could take effect he bounced and the right main gear hit. Now his left wing must be high!

In a smooth motion Chang pulled back the throttles, and the voices of the power plants dropped to a whisper. The brakes! He must put on the brakes before they ran out of what runway they had left. He pressed hard with his toes and felt a near-violent reaction; the nosewheel dropped down and banged onto the runway.

Now the Super-Constellation was running off to the right. He remembered to steer; he whipped his hand down to the wheel at his left knee and twisted it counter-clockwise. The cockpit jerked sharply and he knew he had overdone it. He slacked off and pushed his feet hard on the brakes, his ankles straining to maintain the pressure.

From underneath the aircraft he heard a sound like a muffled explosion, but nothing happened. The landing lights showed a long path of runway still before him; a marker with 6 on it went past.

That meant there were still six thousand feet ahead of him, more than half the runway. At the moment he understood this, he also sensed he was holding the brakes too hard and eased the pressure.

At once things seemed better; the speed had visibly lessened and was now down almost in the Betsy range. He could steer with no further trouble. An ice-cold calm came up through him. He had done it!

He let the aircraft roll on at decreasing speed while he kept the brake pressure moderate and even. He could feel the plane slowing down, and could hear that the engines were only idling. The speed was all gone now; it was only a controlled landing roll. He pressed the brakes just a bit harder and felt the effect at once. He eased off again and saw that they were down almost to taxi speed. To make it smooth and nice he released the brakes almost entirely and let the Super-Constellation roll sedately to a halt.

He looked at Ed and a thin weak grin formed on his lips. Chang sat still, and struggled to smile back.

"Thanks. That was a helluva good flare," Sylvester said finally.

"And a damn good landing, Captain," Chang answered, his voice hoarse. "Now let's taxi this bird in and see where they want us on the ramp."

A light flashed into the cockpit through the windshield and caught Sylvester in the face. Instinctively he closed his eyes. A new voice he had not heard before came into his headset, loud and clear.

"CAP four niner hotel, do not taxi; remain where you are." The words were crisp and definite. Sylvester shaded his eyes, leaned forward, and saw that an emergency vehicle of some kind was on the runway in front of him. That was a damn foolish thing to do, light or no light!

Sylvester pressed the mike button. "I'd like to taxi in," he said. "We have passengers on board."

"Negative," the voice answered. "We know about your passengers. Repeat: do not taxi. You blew a tire on landing."

Sylvester turned toward his partner. "I'm sorry, Ed. I wanted it to be just right, but I guess I messed it up."

"No you didn't," Chang answered promptly. "You set it down perfectly. One of the brakes locked on you on the roll-out, that's all."

Sylvester shook his head. "Nope. I pushed too hard," he admitted. "I thought we were running out of runway and I was frightened."

"Now we're here, I'll tell you—I was petrified," Chang said. "Anything that happens from here on will be an anti-climax."

Sylvester looked over his shoulder toward the ramp. "I'm not so sure of that," he replied. "An awful lot of people seem to be headed our way."

Chapter Fifteen /

DORIS HAD STOOD, HER SLENDER BODY TIGHT, and clung to the fingers of the general's strong hand. The incoming landing lights had seemed to her like the gleaming eyes of some enormous, hypnotic creature, coming relentlessly onward. She'd forced herself to remember that this was an airplane, a fine great modern airliner, bringing Ed nearer every second. Furthermore,. it was his skill that was guiding it home, and she had told herself that he would put it on the runway as well as anybody could do.

Robert Galloway had alternately clenched and unclenched his hands and drummed his fingers against the sides of his legs. He'd told himself that Connie could do it and that a wise old bird like her knew what she was about. At the same time, he'd watched the path of the approaching landing lights and thought that the two kids up on the flight deck were doing a damn fine job. A job he should have done, and then none of the people who surrounded him would have been in this mess.

He'd turned to speak to Herb Stallings and had seen, almost with a shock, that his Constellation pilot was watching the incoming plane with ferocious concentration. "Lower," Herb had said out loud. "Lower!"

The words were not out of his mouth before the lights began to sink slowly below the glide path. "Good," Herb had said. Galloway couldn't help but be reminded of a highly-trained pointer which had sighted game and which was frozen into position, looking ahead.

General Ayms, who felt far from calm himself, had drawn on his long experience and had kept his voice under control. "This looks all right," he'd said to the girl beside him. "Your lieutenant knows what he's doing. He's right on the track and approaching perfectly."

He'd felt the small shoulder underneath his hand relax a fraction of its tension and a little added, grateful pressure from the fingers which gripped his own. "I'm going out to meet them as soon as they have landed," he'd added. "Would you like to come with me?"

The thought was in his mind that if he got her into the car he might be able to spare her a possible sight which would haunt her the rest of her life. He had twice seen men die in crashes and he knew that he would carry the memory of those horrors to his grave.

"Thank you," Doris had answered without turning her face from the incoming aircraft. "As soon as he's landed it safely. I want to see him come in first."

Major Griffin leaned out the window of his staff car. "Sam has cut them loose," he reported. "He feels they will be better on their own now."

"Right," the general answered. "He's done all he could. Pass him my congratulations."

"Yes, sir."

Without looking Doris realized that the ramp was filled with a great many people and vehicles. The lights had come closer so smoothly that it seemed to her as she watched that it was almost supernatural. She stood transfixed as the distance lessened and she could see that the plane itself was almost at the edge of the field. When it came in over the runway lights, she could see its shape and she was startled at its size. She watched with total intensity for the moment when the wheels would touch the ground.

She could not tell the actual contact; instead she saw first that the nose was up in the air and that the plane appeared to be slightly slowing down. Then the nose dropped quite suddenly and the silhouette which she could just make out became level with the ground. That meant that they had landed. Her knees suddenly began to shake violently; she brought her hand up quickly to her mouth because she knew she was going to scream.

The general's fingers tightened into a vise on her shoulder. "Hold it!" he commanded. "They made it. Hang on."

Then she heard Stallings' voice on top of the general's. The pilot spoke with a touch of bitterness. "The damn fool hit the brakes too hard!"

She looked up at the general. "Now?" she asked.

"Right now," the general answered, and held the door open for her.

She did not feel herself get into the car; she only knew

when they started moving, and picked up speed down the ramp toward the other end, where the Constellation stood on the runway.

"Are they all right?" she asked anxiously.

"I'm sure of it," the general answered, warmth in his voice. "We're holding them there where they stopped. They started it, taxied it, took off and flew it, and now they've landed it, but we don't quite trust them to taxi alone at night."

She found herself leaning outward as the staff car turned sharply onto the taxiway. As they swung around she could see that all up and down the huge field a small armada of vehicles was converging toward the now silent plane standing alone against the night. With a shock she realized she had heard almost no sound of the landing; at least she had not been aware of anything but the sight of the landing lights and the long black whalelike shape that had appeared descending out of the sky.

In front of the plane she could see a car of some kind flashing a light up into the cockpit. She looked behind her and saw a parade of staff cars and two police vehicles just turning off the ramp area. It was all confusing to her, but Ed was safe, he was here, and in a few seconds she would see him. That was all that mattered now.

As soon as the Constellation was visibly on the ground the fleet of waiting vehicles on the long ramp began to converge on the point where it would come to rest. The moment it cleared the first taxiway, the fire truck which had been waiting there swung behind it, its deep-throated, powerful engine echoing across the field as it sped in pursuit, red warning lights flashing with full urgency. At the second taxiway a huge crash truck took up the chase with a sleek ambulance racing at its side. Overhead more flashing lights and the sharp slap-slap of the rotors testified that the HH-43B fire-fighting helicopter was above and just behind the slowing airliner.

Before the big bird was fully at rest there was a pattern of headlamps almost at the point on the runway where it would stop. When at last it rolled to a halt and settled back on its landing gear, the helicopter had already set down the fire suppression kit close by and had touched down long enough to permit two absestos-clad rescuemen to jump out of the back. Then it picked up immediately and hovered overhead, ready to direct the powerful downdraft of its twin rotors against any point where fire might break out. Pulling a hose from the kit behind them, the rescuemen ran to the right main gear, where the brakes were smoking and the remnants of the torn tire which still clung to the wheel rim gave off a pungent burning odor.

The driver of another of the big red fire and crash trucks turned onto the runway ahead of the plane and, when the Constellation stopped, directed a strong working light up at the nose section in search of any possible evidence of trouble.

Close behind the general's staff car came Major Griffin in his vehicle. When a full half minute had passed and it was clear there would be no fire, and that the gear was properly locked in the down position, he spoke into his microphone and released the crash trucks from the scene. One by one they backed away and wheeled about to depart. The HH-43B picked up its fire kit after the hose had been recoiled, and flew back to its stand-by position, where it would continue to remain on the alert.

Seeing that several of the vehicles were already beginning

to disgorge a quantity of riders, Griffin called the tower and ordered the Connie to shut down its engines. He waited, wondering if the two unqualified pilots on the flight deck would know how to do that. In a few seconds, almost with visible reluctance, the four propellers, one at a time, swung stiffly to a halt and poised their blades at silent attention. The general, already out of his car, walked briskly the few paces to where Major Griffin was parked. "Get some steps out here," he directed.

"On the way," Griffin answered. An ambulance glided to a stop beside him within a few feet of the rear door of the airliner.

There was a short delay while a stubby tow truck threaded its way past the many parked vehicles, pulling behind it a heavy set of boarding stairs mounted on wheels. As soon as he was as close as he could reasonably come, the driver disengaged the tow bar and swung away to make room. Two airmen who had been riding on the steps proper jumped off, pushed the rolling ramp forward, and maneuvered it carefully into position before the doorway.

Bob Galloway appeared beside the general. "I'd like to send my engineer on board first, to be sure that everything is properly secured," he said, hurrying his words just a little.

"Good idea," Ayms replied.

Galloway nodded to Toolie Sims, who was already waiting at the foot of the stairs. As soon as he had received the signal he started up the steps, two at a time, and opened the fuselage door. There was a reaction as he swung it aside. It could be both heard and felt in the growing group of people gathering at the foot of the ramp. In the very front of the group were two state police officers in uniform, who had automatically taken over partial control; two air policemen were beside them and a lieutenant colonel, who was clearly in charge of the base security forces.

Toolie paused for only a second before he disappeared inside the aircraft. He ignored the crowded load of passengers, nodded quickly to Father Ferrara, who was still standing in the aisle, crowded past him, and made his way rapidly to the flight bridge. As he opened the door to the cockpit he saw the two men in uniform at the controls, who appeared to be trying to complete the after-landing checklist. "Good evening," he said. "I'm Sims." Without further ceremony he seated himself quickly before the flight engineer's panels to go to work.

A quick flash of memory came to Sylvester. "Blackman Sims?" he inquired.

Sims's trained hands were already busy manipulating the controls before him. "Only partly," he answered. "My father was white."

Sylvester didn't know what to say then; Ed Chang picked up the fumble. "Believe me, we're damned glad to have you here to help us. Someone at Tres Santos told us your name was Blackman. Sorry."

Sims was equally fast to accept the apology. "Actually everybody calls me Toolie," he said without stopping his work. Presently he was finished and then he swung around. "Glad to meet you," he added, and held out his hand.

Sylvester, despite his seat belt, which was still fastened, reached quickly to take it first. "Dick Sylvester. My partner, Ed Chang."

Sims shook hands warmly. "I don't know what the others will say," he offered, "but for my part, thank you for saving my airplane."

"You're welcome," Sylvester answered. "I wish you could have been with us."

"You seem to have done all right. Your settings on the final were right on the button."

"Major Aschenbrenner talked us in," Chang said. "He told us what to do."

"Anyhow, you're secured. You might as well start unloading."

"You want us to get off now?" Sylvester asked.

"Why don't you wait a little while?" Sims suggested. "Let the others get off first." With that he turned his back and retreated into the cargo hold.

Without speaking Sylvester released his lap belt, took hold of the seat-release lever, and slid backward to a position where he could climb out of the chair. When he was on his feet he stretched his arms as best he could in the small cockpit and bounced himself once or twice up onto the balls of his feet. "Lord, I'm tired."

Chang slid back and joined him. "I'm with you. At least I could move around a little; you've been sitting there since we took off."

"That was a long time ago," Sylvester added.

"By the way, come back and meet the passengers," Chang suggested.

The muscles of Sylvester's legs were so stiff he almost stumbled as he made his way through the doorway into the hold. The several men there who were on their feet grinned, bowed and nodded. Then Sylvester opened the door to the main cabin.

He had somehow not really believed that there were seventy-eight souls in the back of the aircraft he had been flying, but now he saw them. They were a worn group; some of them were in tears. Father Ferrara spoke quickly in Spanish and there was a very faint cheer from the crowded, tired riders.

"We give you our congratulations and love," the priest said to the pilots. "You have this day saved all of our lives. But we must now at once get a doctor."

"I'm a doctor," a brisk man in uniform said behind him. "Will you let me by, please."

Without ceremony he brushed past, carrying the small black bag of his profession. Immediately behind him a second man, looking very young and in civilian sport clothes, followed.

The little girl who had been burned was crying in deep, chest-racking sobs. "Her clothes caught fire," Chang said as the doctor reached her side.

"I know," the physician answered quickly, and snapped his bag open. He came up with a syringe in his hands and a small bottle of fluid. He filled the needle, held it while he rubbed a spot on her arm with a swab of cotton wet with alcohol, and bending over made a quick, neat injection. Then he rested his hand on the child's forehead and held it there.

Across the aisle the sandy-haired young man had paused only briefly to make a very quick examination of Armando's abdomen; when he touched one point very lightly his patient cried out; immediately after that he was given an injection too.

The doctor in uniform looked up. "Pass the word we need two stretchers," he said. His voice was urgent without being excited.

Father Ferrara nodded at once. "I will tell them," he offered, and moved quickly backward to the doorway.

He had to stoop sharply as he stepped out onto the platform at the top of the steps. When he rose again to his imposing height he could sense the reaction his appearance had created.

"Good night!" the general said softly to the little group that surrounded him. He looked up at the very tall man, who was made taller by the black cassock he wore and taller yet by his position at the top of the stairs. When the priest raised his hand to be heard, he looked to all who saw him like a medieval figure on some great canvas by El Greco. "Two stretchers at once, please," he said—and his words were an anachronism.

"Where did he come from?" Ben Griffin asked, a touch of awe in his voice.

Young Wilson chose his words. "That's Father Ferrara. He's the resident priest for the people in the Tres Santos area. A good man."

The general noted that two litters were being rapidly unloaded from the nearest ambulance and watched while they were carried quickly up the steps and into the aircraft. He felt the expectancy which was beginning to permeate the growing crowd of people gathered around the unloading area. A flash bulb popped, then two more quickly thereafter. The general caught a light, looked to his right, and saw the slim shape of a T-33 rolling down the runway behind the Constellation. He frowned slightly, for a moment disapproving the idea of landing behind a stalled aircraft. Then he realized that Sam Aschenbrenner and his pilot must be all but out of fuel and were therefore justified. He couldn't expect them to go somewhere else, even if they could, and miss the show. Sam had earned a ringside seat.

Father Ferrara bent himself almost double once more and

re-entered the cabin. He spoke a quick sentence in Spanish telling everyone to keep his seat, and then walked up to the front, where the patients were being placed on the litters. "You have given morphine?" he asked.

The doctor in uniform looked up. "No, Father, Demerol. But it has the same effect."

"It is a blessing," the priest said. "A great mercy. Already she is beginning to sleep again."

The doctor snapped his bag shut. "Five minutes is all it needs to start cutting the pain. Will you step aside, Father? Jack wants to get his patient off as soon as possible."

The priest pressed himself out of the way while two attendants lifted Armando onto the ambulance stretcher and held him at shoulder height while they worked their way down the narrow aisle.

"Is he in danger?" Father Ferrara asked the very young doctor in civilian clothes.

"He should be all right, but he needs immediate surgery. I've got to get a consent."

"I give it," the priest said.

The doctor opened his mouth and then closed it again.

"You will operate?" the priest asked.

"Probably within half an hour."

The priest raised his hand and made the sign of the Cross in the air. "God guide your hands," he said. "Are you a Catholic, my son?"

"Lutheran." The doctor started down the aisle.

"God will bless you, none the less." He turned to where the second litter was being picked up with the little girl carefully laid on it. "You will operate also?"

"Probably not," the doctor in uniform answered. "I expect we will send her by Airevac to the Army burn center in

200

Texas. It's a special hospital for cases such as this. If we can get her in, that is."

"It shall be done," the priest said.

The doctor smiled thinly. "It may not be quite that easy, Father, but we'll try."

The priest looked down at him. "We required pilots, God sent them."

"So that's how they made it," the uniformed doctor commented.

"You are not a Catholic either?"

"Jewish, Father. Captain Gordon." He held out his hand.

The priest took it carefully. "You are blessed of God for the work you do. Care for her, she is beloved of us."

"I'll do my best," the captain said and followed the litter down the aisle. Behind his back the tall priest raised his right arm and made a swift sign in the air the captain could not see. Then he followed and watched as the stretcher was carried down the steps.

On the ground the general saw that Major Aschenbrenner, still fresh-looking in his sport jacket and slacks, had joined him. As the litter came down, the general stepped forward for a quick look and saw the relaxed face of the little girl. "That's the burn case, I think," the major said.

"I'm sure of it," Ayms answered. "You did a fine job, Sam. Was it too tough?"

"Bad enough, but those kids who were flying were intelligent types and they did their best." He paused and looked around him. "Which I would say was pretty damn good," he concluded.

The ambulances pulled away; the one bearing Armando turned on its red lights and sped swiftly toward the base hospital.

Robert Galloway joined the small party; behind him Colonel Williams of the Civil Air Patrol came with his two staff officers. Williams quickly shook hands with Aschenbrenner and spoke to him quietly for a moment. Then he performed introductions and Galloway tried to find the proper words to express his thanks to the major who had talked his airplane safely in and onto the ground. He was interrupted by a scene at the doorway of the aircraft.

Father Ferrara and another man in working clothes were helping a very old woman out of the plane. As she carefully felt for her footing she appeared to be at least ninety years of age, a tiny wisp of a woman with a deeply wrinkled face. With greatest care the laborer and the priest helped her slowly down the steps.

"Shall I get . . ." Major Griffin began, but the general silenced him with a gesture. Flash bulbs popped once more. A blue Air Force bus waited in the position which had been vacated by the ambulances.

"Take her to the terminal in my car," the general said. "Have one of our nurses look after her there."

"Yes, sir." Griffin went forward to meet her at the foot of the steps and beckoned the general's driver to draw up.

"Here's another one," Colonel Williams said. They all looked up to see a young woman obviously in the last stages of pregnancy coming out on the arm of her husband. Just as tenderly he guided her down the steps.

"Damn," Aschenbrenner said.

Then the procession began. They came in a long thin line through the doorway, looked about them when they stepped out, and then made their way down the steps. First there were six children of varying ages, then a young mother with a sleeping baby in her arms. Then more children, a flow of adults, and more children. A very heavy-set man made a distinctive appearance as he carried his guitar before him down the steps and then, halfway, opened his mouth in a tremendous smile.

One woman carefully crossed herself as she stepped onto the platform.

And more. People of all ages, some clad in their good clothes, some in their worst. A seemingly never-ending stream of humanity—a little frightened, tired, and uncertain. The first bus filled up and departed for the terminal; the second took its place.

No one in the little executive group had spoken for some time, then Colonel Williams took it upon himself to do so.

"I'm actually proud of them," he said.

Doris Wong silently beamed her gratitude. There was a short pause and then Galloway added, "Well, so am I."

Toolie Sims felt the mood in the air. "If they made any serious mistakes, I didn't see them," he contributed. "They had everything set right when I checked the board."

"How were they?" the general asked.

"Tired—but on their feet."

General Ayms looked at Colonel Williams. "Are you going to reprimand them?" he inquired.

"Well—I've been considering that, but in view of what I've seen and heard I'm going to call it in line of duty. A little overzealous, perhaps, but when I saw that little girl I think I understood why they did it. I might have done the same."

"Mr. Galloway?" the general asked.

Bob spoke without looking away from the Constellation.

"They took my airplane without permission, but they also saved it from probable destruction. I'll pay for the tire. Also your tab here if I can afford it."

The general turned to Aschenbrenner. "They did declare an emergency, didn't they, Sam?"

"Yes, sir, absolutely they did. As soon as they discovered that the elevator control was inoperative. They hadn't determined that before take-off, of course."

"In that case they had a right to ask for our help," General Ayms said.

The lieutenant colonel who was the provost marshal spoke up. "Do you have any further need for my boys, sir?"

The people were still streaming slowly off the aircraft. There seemed to be no end to them.

The commander thought quietly for a moment. When he spoke his voice was flat and unemotional. "I don't think so, Mike. That goes for the state police and the FBI people too, that is as far as we're concerned. Immigration and Public Health are another matter, of course."

"Sir," Griffin cut in, "some of the press boys are asking for a statement."

"Tell them we received a call from an airliner in distress and responded as we always do under such circumstances. The landing was fortunately routine and that's all there was to it. No casualties. Some passengers who were ill are being cared for until they can be moved to an appropriate civilian facility."

"Passengers, sir?"

"Correction—evacuees."

"Yes, sir, I'll pass the word."

General Ayms turned to Aschenbrenner. "Sam, do you

know what we forgot? We should have set up some messing facilities for this many people."

Sam Aschenbrenner replied. "I think Ben Griffin anticipated your order in that regard, sir. He said he has a chow line set up and quarters arranged too, I believe. That's authorized, sir, since these people are evacuees from a disaster area."

"True," the general said. "Ben knows his job."

"Yes, sir," Aschenbrenner said. "He does."

"I think that's the last of them," Herb Stallings interjected. He had remained silent for so long the others had all but forgotten he was there.

"Permission to go on board, sir?" Aschenbrenner asked.

"Go ahead," the general said.

Aschenbrenner ran lightly up the steps and was halfway up the aisle of the now empty cabin when the door to the cargo hold again opened and Captain Sylvester came through.

"Hello, Dick," the major said.

"Hello, sir," Sylvester answered. His voice showed a touch of unsteadiness. "You're Major Aschenbrenner, aren't you."

Sam Aschenbrenner held out his hand; Sylvester took it as Ed Chang came through the doorway from the hold. "Gentlemen," Aschenbrenner said. "The bar is open at the officers' club and also I realize you haven't had dinner. Would you care to join me?"

"We'd be honored, sir, but we have the feeling that we just may be in a little trouble. That could detain us," Sylvester said grimly. "Also I saw Colonel Williams, our C.O., out there, and we have to report to him of course. I'm sorry—this is Ed Chang."

The major reached out and shook hands firmly with the slimly built lieutenant. Then he turned and led the way out of the aircraft. When he was outside he hurried noticeably down the steps so that when Sylvester came through the doorway of the aircraft the steps were clear.

Sylvester took hold of the rail and looked down at all of the people and vehicles. The second of the blue Air Force buses was pulling away toward the terminal, the crash trucks had long since departed, but there was still a sizeable reception committee. He lifted his chin and prepared to walk down the steps. Then he moved aside to give Ed Chang room and waited until his partner was with him.

Several flash bulbs exploded bursts of light into their faces. A flood lamp came on so brilliantly they could hardly see. Ed Chang shaded his eyes and saw that it was being held next to a movie cameraman who was apparently taking their picture.

Sylvester started down the steps with Chang a step behind him. He wanted desperately to look back at the long shape of the airliner they had just landed, but he knew that he had an obligation to maintain a military bearing. He was a civilian, but he was in the uniform of the Civil Air Patrol, on a United States Air Force base, and his colonel was watching him.

When he reached the ground he waited a moment until Chang was beside him, then he walked up to Colonel Williams and saluted.

"Good evening, sir," he said, and waited.

GLOSSARY

As an aid to those readers who may not be familiar with technical aviation terms, the following definitions may be helpful in following the flight of Captain Sylvester and Lieutenant Chang.

A/C • Aircraft commander, the pilot in charge.

AILERONS • Small movable control surfaces at the wingtips used when banking an aircraft right or left.

AIREVAC • Air evacuation, a flying ambulance service maintained and operated by the Military Airlift Command.

AOK • An expression meaning that everything is functioning well.

AP • Air Police, the law enforcement arm of the Air Force.

ARS • Air Rescue Service, an invaluable part of the Military Airlift Command.

ARTIFICIAL HORIZON • A flight instrument which provides the pilot with a visual indication of the real horizon at night or under adverse weather conditions.

ATC • Air Traffic Control.

BALLOON • To surge upward while in flight.

BIRD DOG • A radio navigation device which points visually toward any station within range to which it is tuned.

BUY THE FARM • An airmen's term meaning to crash fatally.

C-47 • Military designation for the Douglas DC-3.

C-121 • Military designation for the Lockheed Constellation. C-121G is the Super-Constellation. In common speech C-121 is taken to mean any of this particular breed of airplane.

CG • Center of Gravity.

CHECKLIST • Standard lists of items which must be checked and verified during various phases of flight.

COMMAND SET • A multi-channel radio transceiver which can operate on several different frequencies.

CROSSWIND • Wind which is blowing across a runway making it difficult, or impossible, for aircraft to operate from that strip.

DME • Distance Measuring Equipment. A radio navigational aid which indicates numerically the distance in nautical miles to certain transmitting facilities.

E6B • A navigational computer extensively used in World War II and still highly efficient for most missions.

ETA • Estimated Time of Arrival.

FIREWALL • The forward bulkhead of the cockpit, so named because in single-engined craft it is literally a fire barrier between the powerplant and the airframe.

FIVE BY FIVE • A description of the quality of radio reception. The scale runs from one to five and covers volume and readability. Five by five, therefore, means with maximum volume and clarity. Four by four is slightly inferior in both categories, but still satisfactory for communications.

FLAPS • Supplementary movable surfaces which, when lowered, increase the lift of the wings at the price of increased drag. They are used only at slower speeds.

FLARE • A maneuver used in landing an aircraft. It consists of breaking the descending speed and raising the nose of the plane into a touchdown attitude.

FLIGHT PLAN • A report, filed by a pilot to indicate when he is going, by what route, and when he expects to arrive. It is monitored by air traffic control; if the plane fails to appear as expected, shortly thereafter search and rescue operations are set in motion.

FSK • Fire Suppression Kit.

GCA • Ground Control Approach, a precision radar system used in landing aircraft under adverse conditions.

GLIDE SLOPE INDICATOR • A device which informs a landing pilot how far he is above or below the ideal path from his altitude to the end of the runway.

GO JUICE • Gasoline or other aviation fuel.

GOONIE • Also Goonie Bird, an affectionate name for the indestructible DC-3.

GROUND LOOP • A sudden turn, intentional or otherwise, by an aircraft near the end of its landing roll.

HEAD • The Navy word for toilet, which is frequently used by the other services.

HH-43B • A powerful, turbine-powered helicopter used in fire-fighting and rescue work.

ID • Identification.

IFR • Instrument Flight Rules. To fly under these conditions requires special training and an appropriate license.

ILS • Instrument Landing System, a radio navigational aid which is of great help in bringing aircraft in for landings during conditions of poor visibility.

INCHES • The amount of power being delivered by an engine as measured by manifold pressure in terms of inches of mercury.

INDICATED • The speed as shown by the air speed indicator in an aircraft. Because of varying pressures and atmospheric conditions, it is usually an understatement of the true air speed.

IO • Information Officer, the public relations representative of a military body.

KEY • A term used in the Caribbean area to signify a small island.

L-6 • A light, two-place utility aircraft formerly built by Interstate. They have been out of production for some time.

MAGNETIC HEADING • A direction indicated by a magnetic compass which is based on magnetic north, not true north.

MEAT WAGON • Ambulance.

NINER • The standard way of pronouncing the numeral nine for greater clarity in radio transmission.

OMNI • A standard radio navigational system which replaced the old low-frequency "range leg" technique.

OPS • Operations.

P & W • Pratt and Whitney, a leading manufacturer of aircraft engines.

PAX • Passengers.

PHILLIPS • A special type of screw head or driver which utilizes a cross slot.

POWER CURVE • The amount of power being delivered by an aircraft's engines measured against the drag which must be overcome. Getting on the wrong side of the power curve is an invitation to disaster.

RED-LINE • Used as a verb, to certify an aircraft as unsafe for flight.

RED TAG • A tag, real or figurative, which is attached to the controls of an aircraft when it is unsafe to fly.

SOP • Standard Operating Procedure.

T-BIRD • A familiar designation for the Lockheed T-33 jet trainer.

TAIL NUMBER • The individual designating number of a military aircraft which is normally painted on its tail.

TRANSPONDER • An electronic device installed in larger aircraft. It is used to send out identifying code signals which are visible on radar scopes.

TRIM TAB • A small device installed on the control surfaces of an aircraft to permit minor adjustments of dynamic balance. They are, in effect, very small control surfaces, but they can sometimes be employed to move the larger surfaces to which they are customarily attached.

TURBOPROP • An aircraft, or aircraft power plant, which employs a turbine engine to turn a propeller. It is a cross between a conventional piston-engine-propeller combination and a pure jet.

U-2 • A Lockheed aircraft capable of very high altitude flight.

U-3A • Military designation for the Cessna 310 aircraft. It is a small twin-engine plane which will carry five persons.

VFR • Pronounced Victor Foxtrot Romeo in radio transmissions, this abbreviation stands for Visual Flight Rules. In essence it means flying by eyesight without the aid of special instruments or sophisticated electronic navigational aids.

VHF • Very High Frequency.

VOR • Visual Omni Range, an electronic system which points the way to the nearest omni station.

VORTAC • VOR combined with Tactical Air Navigation, in effect a longer-range VOR.

WEATHERCOCK • The involuntary turning of an aircraft into the wind, with the tail surfaces acting roughly like the feathers on an arrow.

WEIGHT AND BALANCE • A calculation normally made before a large aircraft takes off to assure the fact that it is not overloaded and that the center of gravity is within allowable limits.

WILCO • Will comply.

YANKEE ROUTE • A primary air route on the eastern side of the Caribbean.

YOKE • A term commonly applied to the control wheel of a larger aircraft and to the support to which it is attached. In earlier designs this structure often was in yoke form. The term applies to the pilot's and co-pilot's controls together.